Mate of the Phoenix

C.A. VARIAN

Editing by Willow Oak Author Services

Page Edge Design by Painted Wings Publishing

Cover Design by Fay Lane

Hardcase Design by D'Arte Oriel

Color Edition Cover Design by D'Arte Oriel

Chapter Designs by Leigh Cover Designs

2nd Edition 2024

2nd Edition 2025

CONTENTS

TRIGGER WARNING

There are mature themes throughout this book, and it is not intended for readers under 17 years of age.

The following themes are explored in Mate of the Phoenix: Graphic (consensual) sexual content, captivity, slavery, abduction, vulgar language, and murder.

EKOTORIA

Aegricia
Marella Arch
Norithae
Spectre Forest
Elder Sea
Undying Desert
Diapolis
Warbotach

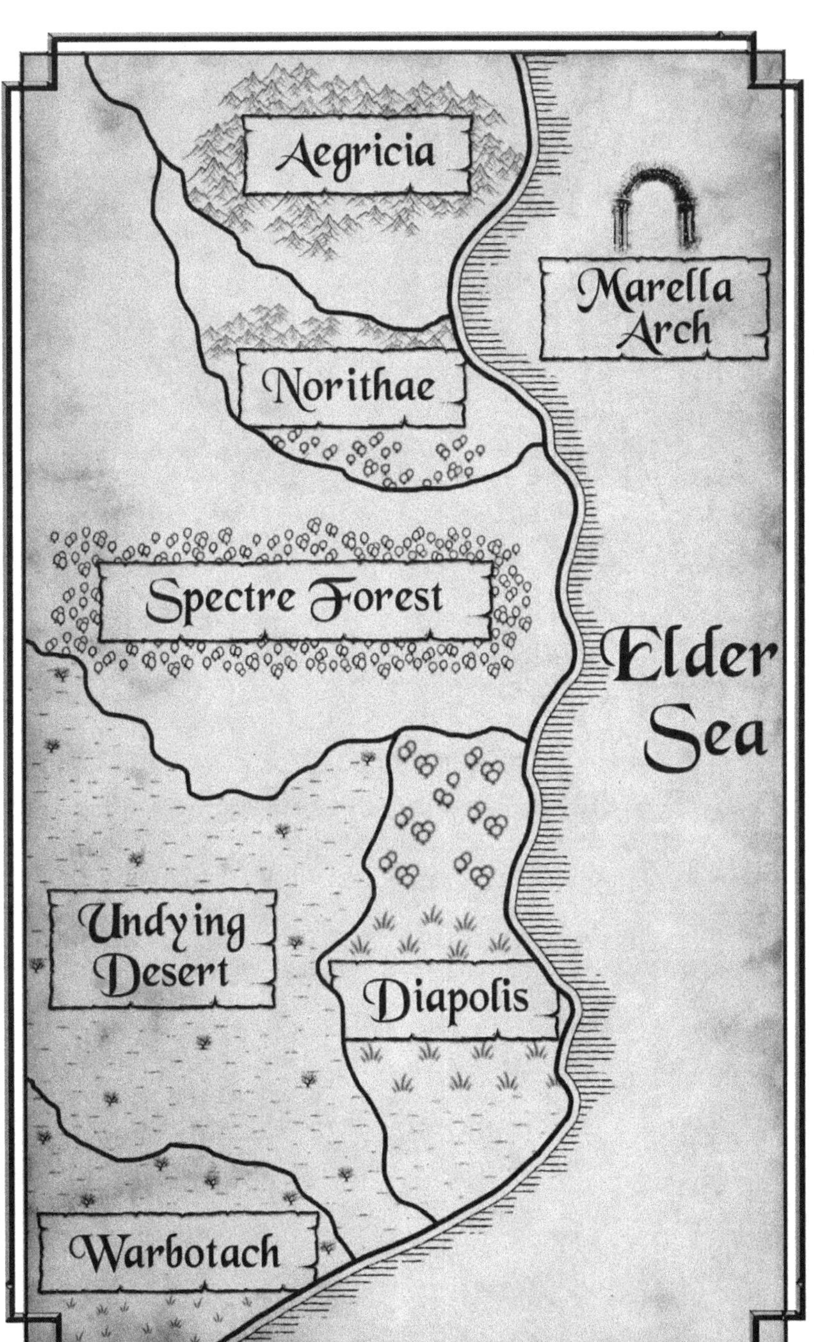

HOLERA

"What are you doing tonight?"

Holera Glowbrook pulled her bowstring taut and took aim, hitting the bullseye on a target that was more than one thousand yards away while waiting for her friend to answer. She barely allowed herself a nod. Anything less than perfection wasn't worth noting, and she'd sooner scowl than gloat. Even in the ranks of hundreds of Aegrician warriors, she was one of the best with a bow.

Her best friend, Exie Cinderdraft, whistled as she eyed the target. Her whistle was so loud a pair of rookies two rings over startled and dropped their arrows. Exie only grinned, unbothered as always. "Heading to the Singing Lantern. You?"

"No plans yet." Holera lifted a brow, her tone dry. "Hot date?" She was not at all surprised that Exie planned to go to the tavern. Unlike her, Exie liked to go out and be sociable. Holera, on the other hand,

had been spending too many nights in silence—the kind where even her mother's steady stitching by the hearth couldn't drown out the ache of loneliness.

Exie barked a laugh, her long, blond mane flailing forward as it always did when she was being overly dramatic. "No. I don't have a date. Do you want to come with me? You rarely go out anymore."

Of course her friend was correct. Their military training had been rigorous so, although Exie still had energy when they were done for the day, Holera didn't. Exie could spar all day and still find the strength to drink and flirt. Holera, meanwhile, felt every bruise settling into her muscles. It may have been all in her head. She realized that. Ever since her father had died, she'd had less desire to socialize with anyone aside from Exie, and even her patience for that had been limited. Grief had made her quieter, sharper around the edges. Some days she feared she'd carved herself into stone, with only Exie loud enough to chip at the surface.

Both she and Exie were phoenix shifters. All the Aegrician female warriors were. But unlike the others, who were serious more often than not, Exie spent most of her time with a lighthearted exuberance about her that was infectious, or completely annoying. Yet when trouble came, Exie was the first to throw herself into it, wild grin and blade flashing. Loyalty burned hotter in her than whiskey. Still, staying home every night with her mother who spent her own time making clothing, had become more than lonely for Holera. She was still young, and she longed for a steady hand at her back, a voice that spoke her name like it mattered. But all she had was empty nights and the rasp of thread through cloth.

She nodded, but with a sardonic smile. Her tone was flat as steel, though the corner of her mouth betrayed her amusement. "I'll go with you, but the minute you start building your harem, I'm out of there."

It only took Exie a second to laugh again, smacking Holera hard on the back, nearly knocking the bow out of her hand. Holera grunted and barely kept from snarling — Exie's affection always came with bruises. "Deal, but my harem does need building."

Holera had no response to that but an eye roll.

The friends left the training ring after their discussion, fire erupting from their skin as they shifted into phoenix form. Heat rippled the air before their wings caught the sky, carrying them in opposite directions. Exie shot off toward the heart of Flamecliff, reckless arcs of rainbow fire lighting her path, while Holera angled north, her silver wings steady and sharp.

Although they both lived near the capital, their homes couldn't have been more different. Exie kept a cramped apartment above the main square, close to the taverns and the pulse of the city. Holera preferred the quiet edge of the world, sharing a small cottage with her mother on the outskirts. Quiet didn't always mean peace. Sometimes it felt like exile. Still, after a day of sweat and dust, she would rather face silence than walk into a tavern stinking of training leathers and send the entire crowd running from her stench.

Aegricia—the kingdom Holera called home—was the northernmost realm of Ekotoria. It was the cradle of phoenix shifters, though not every Aegrician carried fire in their veins. Only women chosen for the warrior class could shift into flame and wing; the rest of Aegricia's people, men and non-warrior women alike, kept their fae forms. Holera still remembered the first time her skin had ignited and feathers had replaced flesh. Terrifying. Exhilarating. The mark that she was destined to fight.

The warriors of Aegricia guarded the Marella portal, a jagged arch of sea glass where the cliffs met the Elder Sea. It connected their world to the human one, though neither side had crossed in generations. Treaties held. Laws held. But the portal still pulsed with magic, whether mortals respected it or not. The only way across was on the wings of a phoenix—or clinging to the back of one—and so the burden of protection rested squarely on Holera's kind. She doubted she'd ever see a human brave the crossing, yet still she knew: guarding the portal was the greatest honor their kingdom could give.

South of Aegricia lay Norithae. Its people were all born with leathery wings, every man, woman, and child. Holera thought it unfairly convenient. Aegricians had to earn their fire.

Most of the continent's center was swallowed by Spectre Forest. Plenty of fae had crossed it, though few bothered to linger. The farther in one went, the stranger and darker the beasts became — reason enough, in Holera's mind, to steer clear.

On Ekotoria's southeastern edge lay Diapolis. Holera had never flown so far, though she often dreamed of the warmth there. It was said that dragons still curled in its volcanic peaks, and that its people could slip into the sea, trading legs for shimmering tails. Even in Aegricia's cold taverns, travelers spoke of Diapolis with awe, their voices painting it bright as a jewel in her imagination. One day, she promised herself.

The opposite corner of the continent held only ruin. The Undying Valley crept outward year by year, its sands devouring farmland and rivers until little remained of the once-fertile southwest. Warbotach clung to what scraps were left, a kingdom of barbarians penned into a shrinking corner by desert and sea. Their king was said to be cruel. Their warriors, vicious. Holera had no wish to test the rumors. She prayed she never would.

By the time she reached the outskirts of Flamecliff, the sky had turned into a sweep of orange, pink, and purple. She landed in front of her mother's cottage in a flare of silver flame, boots crunching on packed snow as her wings folded into nothing. The mountains rose behind the city, jagged and white, their crowns eternal in snow, their distance untouchable to all but the gods. Holera lingered, watching the younger phoenix warriors wheel in perfect formation above a lower ridge. Show-offs, she thought with a smirk, though pride still swelled in her chest. Training drills or not, they made the sky beautiful.

Chapter Two

HOLERA

Thanks to the fae magic within their city, most dwellings had heated water that came from the tap. In Flamecliff proper, pipes hissed with enchanted steam. Out here, on the edge of the wilds, Holera and her mother relied on firewood and patience.

Kissing her mother on the forehead, Holera added water to the pot hanging from the mantle and heated it for her bath. Her mother smelled faintly of lavender and smoke, a comfort Holera had never outgrown. Her fighting leathers reeked of sweat and dirt, as did her long, silver locks. Tossing the soiled clothing to the floor, she lowered herself into the copper tub. Sweat, leather, and ash clung to her until the bathwater steamed around her skin, carrying the day's grime away. She ducked beneath the surface and soaped her hair, groaning at the way the hot water loosened every knot in her muscles.

For a moment, she debated staying home. Why bother going out to watch Exie sing off-key and drink herself stupid? Exie had plenty of friends to keep her company. But Exie wanted *her* company, and that was reason enough. Holera might complain, but she would never leave her friend to drink alone.

So, pushing her hesitation aside, she climbed from the bath, dried her body with a cloth, and pulled on a tunic over damp skin and a pair of trousers. No gowns, no frills—just the armor of a warrior who couldn't quite pretend to be anything else.

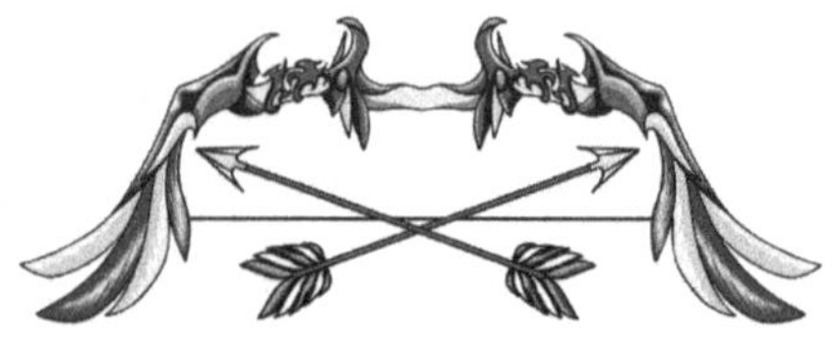

After flying into the city proper, Holera's silver hair was still wet when she shifted back into her fae form, so she pulled it into a braid as she approached the log entrance of the Singing Lantern Tavern. Sounds of the tavern's revelry assaulted her before she even had a chance to open the heavy wooden door. Fiddle strings screeched over the roar of laughter, and the sour-sweet smell of spilled ale hit her nose. Her hand hesitated on the handle. Why she ever let Exie drag her into places like this, she'd never know. But then a familiar voice rose above the din, sharp with fury. Exie sounded like she was about to get into a fight.

Darting into the building, the door slamming behind her, Holera spotted her best friend near the bar, hair disheveled and a scowl on her face, squared off against a large male with an eye patch. Exie's wild blond mane clung to the sweat on her brow, her scowl promising violence. Holera's long legs carried her across the room in a few strides, and she wedged herself between them, face set in an exasperated scowl. At times she felt less like Exie's equal and more like the keeper of her chaos.

"What's going on, Ex? I can hear you screaming like a hellhound from outside!"

The man grumbled behind her before slinking away. Holera barely spared him a glance before turning back to her friend. Exie was taller and more muscular than she was, and Holera never found her intimidating—until she was angry.

"That Warbotach scum was insulting our queen!" Leaning around Holera's form, Exie shouted to the room at large. "He needs to grab the rest of his bandit crew, get back on his ship, and go back to his own damn kingdom."

The crowd bristled. Tankards stilled. A few muttered curses hissed through teeth. As if Exie's words had carried weight—or maybe it was the harsh stares of the Aegrician locals—but the group of stout, scarred Warbotach men filed out. Exie smirked in triumph.

Holera tipped her chin at the barmaid, silent but firm. A drink in each hand was the fastest way to keep Exie from storming after them. Forcing her friend into a chair, she slid a mug of Aegrician whiskey across the bar. Thankfully, the busy woman dropped two steaming mugs of the liquid fire before them a moment later.

"Were you just going to take on them all, Exie? You may be tough, but every one of those men were beasts."

Exie grinned, taking a deep draw of her whiskey, her eyes already glassy with drink. "The rest of the bar would've joined in the fight. I wasn't scared of them." Her grin widened, sharp as a blade. She'd fight the whole world if it meant defending Otera's name.

Holera caught her wrist before she could raise the mug again, exhaling through clenched teeth. "I would've stayed home if I'd known you were going to be in here starting fights." Bathing was wasted effort if she was just going to end up mopping up after Exie.

Exie's eyes widened at her tone. She lowered her hand, her features softening. "You're right, you're right. I'll calm down. I promise."

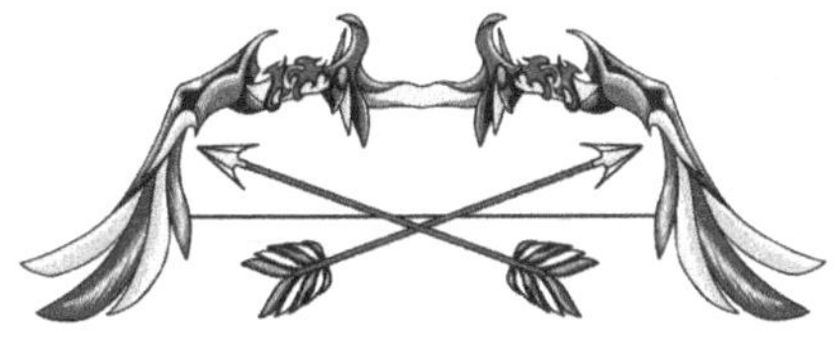

After an hour of watching her best friend sing along with the band, it was clear Exie hadn't calmed down, but at least she was happy. Holera leaned against the bar, watching as the intoxicated warrior sang song after song, adding lyrics wherever she saw necessary, but the band didn't seem to mind. Patrons roared with laughter, tankards pounding the tables in rhythm. Exie soaked in the attention like fire taking to dry kindling.

"Your friend is…um…lively."

Unbeknownst to Holera, a male had taken the stool next to her, ordering a whiskey from the barmaid. Holera stiffened, ready to elbow whoever dared invade her space—until she caught the green of his eyes. His long, black hair was pulled back with a leather cord at his nape. Rolled up to the elbows, his heavy white tunic strained against his muscled arms and chest, dark tattoos peeking through where the fabric failed to cover. The mischievous sparkle in his green eyes was a stark contrast to his fierce appearance.

Holera smirked. "That is certainly an understatement." Although she hadn't necessarily gone to the tavern to find a male, she couldn't deny how sexy this one was, so she didn't move away. Trust her luck to meet someone like him on a night she smelled of sweat, ale, and Exie's bad decisions. If anything, she could soak in the view of him and think about him when she slipped her hand between her thighs that night. It had been such a long time since she'd found pleasure.

"Warrior?" His question caught her by surprise, her head tilting.

"Hrmm?"

Taking a sip of his drink, he set it back down on the bar. "I asked if you and your friend were warriors. Sorry to pry. If you were, I just wanted to thank you for your bravery."

"Oh." She grinned, a flush coloring her cheeks. "We are, but you don't have to thank us." She pointed behind herself where the shadow of a silver wing flared out of her back. Silver fire shimmered faintly in the darkness, a reminder of what she was born to be. "I was born this way, after all."

Grunting his acknowledgement, he took another sip of his whiskey and smiled. "Well, I still admire the warriors of this land. I've been all over the continent, but none are as fierce as Aegricia's."

Pride tugged at her, though she tried to smother it beneath a scowl. She couldn't help but smile at his compliment before dropping her face into something more neutral when she realized she was starting to behave like a flirty young maiden, which she certainly was not.

Just as she was about to thank him again, Exie grabbed her by the arm and pulled her toward the exit. All she could do was glance back at him as the door closed behind her, blocking him from view. She hadn't even gotten his name.

"What's going on, Ex?" Before her friend could respond, Exie pulled Holera around the side of the building where the blond warrior retched, the whiskey finally taking its revenge on her stomach. Holera held back Exie's wild mane, careful to keep it out of her friend's face. Exie could pick fights with a whole ship of Warbotach, yet lose to a bottle of whiskey. If she hadn't regretted going to the tavern before, she was beginning to as Exie stood, only to wobble on shaky legs.

"Come on, let's get you home."

Thanks to Exie's inebriated state, Holera didn't dare leave her to fly back to her cottage. She hoped her mother wouldn't worry, but her mother was probably already asleep. Holera was more concerned her friend would get herself into trouble if she left her alone. In the morning, she would need to have a conversation with Exie about her behavior. Her best friend, already unconscious on her bed, was not in the right frame of mind for a lecture. So, only slightly grumbling under her breath, Holera grabbed an extra blanket from a wooden chest and settled down on the sofa, still thinking about the sexy male from the bar. She wondered if she'd ever see him again and hoped she would. Not that she'd admit it to Exie—or even herself.

CHAPTER THREE
HOLERA

"Get up, Ex. We're going to be late." Holera shook her friend's shoulders, but all she got was a whine and a groan. Exie's hangovers were infamous. Holera had survived enough of them to know they came with whining, swearing, and at least one dramatic declaration of impending death.

"Go without me." Exie's voice was muffled by the pillow, but her tone was beyond dramatic. Holera pulled the pillow out of her friend's grasp, swatting her on the back with it. If she didn't drag Exie to training, she'd end up cleaning blood out of the woman's tunics when Blaedia punished her.

"Blaedia would kill you if you didn't show up to training. Going without you isn't an option, and you know it."

Tossing off her blankets, Exie climbed out of bed, but not without a string of swear words as she did. "Just for the record, I'm only getting up so Blaedia doesn't

kill me." Her voice carried the same theatrical weight she used when singing with the tavern band — as though the gods themselves needed to hear her suffering.

"Noted. Oh, I'm going to need some fighting leathers, since I was forced to stay at your place last night."

Exie shot Holera a sideways glance. "First of all, you didn't have to stay. I would've been just fine. Second of all, my clothes would swallow you whole. But, if you still want to wear them, they're in the first drawer on the right."

Holera didn't even bother reminding her friend that she had no choice but to stay because someone had to watch over her in her drunken stupor. Instead of responding, she let it go and grabbed a set of leathers from Exie's dresser, pulling them on although they were absolutely too large. The sleeves nearly swallowed her hands, and she scowled at how ridiculous she must look. Exie would find it hilarious. Holera found it humiliating.

"You look like a fledgling drowning in her mother's cloak," Exie croaked with a grin.

Holera grunted and tugged the belt tighter. "Laugh it up. If I faint from embarrassment in front of Blaedia, it's your fault."

The two phoenix warriors arrived at the training camp fifteen minutes later than they were expected, earning an icy blue glare from their general, Blaedia. Even from across the yard, that glare could strip flesh from bone. With her chin-length, razor-straight black hair shaved on one side, she looked every inch the blade she wielded, her posture sharp and her movements disciplined, danger coiled in every line of her body. She was Queen Otera's lover, but that wasn't how she'd earned such a high-ranking position. Blaedia had traveled throughout the continent, learning military strategy and techniques from the best generals in Ekotoria, and she had returned to lead Aegricia's military. Her warriors knew tardiness was not something she tolerated, so Holera clenched her teeth as they shifted, hoping they wouldn't get into trouble.

The clang of steel rang through the valley, sweat and dust hanging thick in the air as rookies stumbled through drills under the unforgiving sun. To Holera's relief, their general was fully involved in a training exercise with the younger warriors and didn't approach them to give them a piece of her mind. The look on her face said enough.

Hoping to lessen the blow, Holera drew her sword and pointed it at Exie. If Blaedia was going to skin them alive for tardiness, Holera could at least pretend they'd been training all along.

At the first slash of her sword, Exie jumped back with a screech. Her voice cracked so loudly it startled a pair of rookies in the next ring. "You could at least warn me first!" She drew her own weapon, her movements slow and awkward from the late night of drinking as she held it out in front of her. "Some friend you are."

Huffing a breath, Holera circled her. Exie followed her movements and waited for the next strike. "I was a good enough friend to stay with you last night." She lunged, her weapon swinging toward Exie's vulnerable left side, only to be met midair by her friend's blade.

Chuckling, the hungover warrior feigned to the right but slashed to the left. Holera didn't fall for her bluff. Unlike Exie, her senses weren't dulled by the overabundance of whiskey the night before. "I don't think this is about you having to deal with me last night at all." Exie swung again, Holera's blade meeting hers with a clang. "This is because I pulled you out of the tavern before you could take that sexy male you were talking to back to your bed."

Holera tried to deny it with her face, rolling her eyes as she dodged another blow, but there was no way to hide anything from her best friend. Exie knew her too well. She hadn't planned to bring him back to her bed, at least not last night, but she hadn't gotten his face out of her mind since she'd left the tavern. There was something about him she couldn't forget, even if she knew little about him.

"I wasn't going to take him to my bed." Her words were less than convincing, but she still decided to go all in anyway as she pivoted out of the way of Exie's sword. "Besides, my mom would murder me if I brought some strange male home while she was sleeping. The cabin is way too small."

Throwing her head back in her usual dramatic fashion, Exie laughed, her sword limp in her hand. Holera took the opening and swung, knocking her friend's weapon to the ground. Too wrapped up in her laughter, Exie didn't even notice. "So you did want to take him to your bed, but you didn't want your mother to hear?"

Unable to deny it, Holera shrugged and plopped down on the ground, lack of sleep catching up with her in the heat of the midday sun. Aegricia was colder than most of the continent, but the valley in which they trained lacked the tree cover of the southern side of the mountain range.

When her friend sat beside her, their weapons on the ground instead of in their hands, Holera knew they were going to be in trouble with their general but didn't care enough to stand and keep sparring. Loosening a breath, she wrapped her arms tightly around her bent knees and watched a group of young phoenixes fly into the mountain pass.

For once, Exie's grin faltered. "Theoni would've laughed at all this, you know. Called me reckless and kissed me anyway." Her voice dropped, softer than Holera was used to. "Sometimes I wonder if I'll ever stop hearing her."

Holera turned, her chest tightening at the rare glimpse beneath her friend's bravado, but before she could respond, Exie gave a sharp toss of her blond mane. The grin snapped back into place, armor as quick as any blade. "But since I can't, you're stuck with me."

"It doesn't matter. I'll probably never see him again." Saying it aloud made Holera's chest twist, as if she'd confessed a weakness she hadn't meant to share. Her need for a true companion was clearly deeper than she wanted to admit.

Exie leaned forward and rested her elbows on her knees, her playful laughter gone. "Did you at least find out where he was from? Maybe you could track him down." Her tone was light, but the gleam in her eye said she'd gladly help, if Holera only asked.

"I didn't even get his name. I was a little too preoccupied with you." She arched an eyebrow in Exie's direction, but her friend had turned away, watching as Blaedia approached from the direction of the training rings.

"Oh," Holera groaned under her breath as she stood, dusting off her leathers before reaching out a hand to Exie.

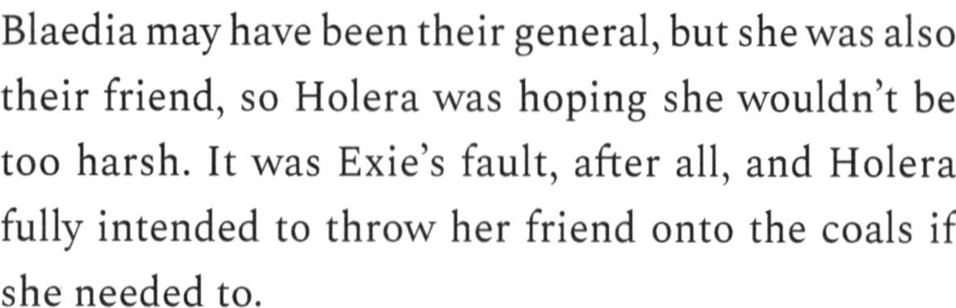

Blaedia may have been their general, but she was also their friend, so Holera was hoping she wouldn't be too harsh. It was Exie's fault, after all, and Holera fully intended to throw her friend onto the coals if she needed to.

Holera

Holera cringed inwardly but tried to keep a neutral face as her general stepped in front of her, knowing she and Exie's tardiness hadn't gone unnoticed. Two young warriors trailing behind her, the females no older than their teens, Blaedia's glare could have ended wars. Holera's stomach twisted. She'd rather face a Warbotach warband than that look.

"Glad you found time to come to training today, although—" She paused for impact, pulling a small dagger out of its sheath and using it to clean her nails. "You haven't done much training since you got here."

Tilting her head toward Exie, Holera cleared her throat, shoving her friend over the coals indeed. Blaedia didn't miss the gesture and arched an eyebrow at her as well.

"Do I need to ask why one of my best warriors tried to start a fight in the tavern last night?"

The two young warriors flanking Blaedia failed to hide their snickers, but the general didn't turn her attention away from Exie.

"They insulted Otera."

Blaedia lifted an eyebrow, incredulity clear on her face. "What did they say to insult Otera?"

Kicking at the pebbles at her feet, Exie looked like a child who was being scolded by its mother. Which, in a way, she was. Blaedia had raised half the army by glare alone.

"They praised Joneira, called her the rightful queen."

Blaedia stiffened. Joneira, the usurper queen, was a sensitive topic for all Aegricians. She'd killed the previous queen, Otera's grandmother, and had stolen the throne for a short period of time before she was forced out of the kingdom. The name Joneira still echoed through Aegricia like a curse. Holera hated even hearing it spoken aloud.

"Did they?" Although her face showed no emotion, Holera could tell Blaedia was still frazzled. "Well, let's hope they don't return to this kingdom then."

When Blaedia tipped her head toward the young phoenixes, giving them a nonverbal direction,

Holera knew their punishment was coming. She swallowed, waiting for it.

"These young warriors need some practice with the bow. The two of you," she said, leveling her eyes at Holera and Exie, "will collect their arrows."

Holera let out a breath, relief washing over her. Collecting stray arrows wasn't as bad of a punishment as they could've been given. Tedious, but not difficult. If all they had to do was chase after fledglings' missed shots, she could endure the humiliation. At least it wasn't latrine duty.

Exie nodded, no argument on her tongue. As Blaedia began walking away, she turned to look over her shoulder. "Otera's having a party tonight. There are some emissaries here for a meeting. The two of you are coming."

There it was. The punishment. None of them liked going to court, hated it actually. Blaedia didn't want to go, but she had no choice. She and Otera were lovers, mates even. Since she had to suffer through it, she wanted them to as well. Exie may have been quiet about chasing arrows, but she groaned at this. Holera couldn't blame her. A night at court was worse than chasing a hundred stray arrows. Not that it would make any difference. They weren't going to get out of it.

As Blaedia walked away, with a noticeable strut in her step, Holera could have sworn she heard the general chuckle. Holera blinked. Blaedia never chuckled. Which meant their misery was entertaining her more than it should have.

The archery practice for the two young warriors lasted for two hours, and they hadn't taken it easy on Holera and Exie. Instead of aiming at set targets, where the arrows would all land on relatively flat soil nearby, they darted around, shooting at everything under the sun. Holera was half-convinced the fledglings aimed for the muddiest ground they could find just to watch her scramble. Trees, boulders, a scurrying critter—the young warriors found joy in making them chase every last shaft.

By the time they'd tired out and most of their arrows had been broken, Holera was drenched in sweat and covered in filth. Sweat plastered her tunic to her back, and twigs clung to her braids as though the forest itself had joined in mocking her. Shooting her friend a few thoughtful glares, she shifted into her phoenix form and left the training field for her mother's cottage. If she was going to attend court, she needed a bath and a clean set of clothes.

Having not returned home the night before, she'd expected her mother to be a little more worried than she was, but she found her mother where she'd always been—sitting in her chair by the fire, contentment on her face.

"Glad you found your way home, wildfire. Late night?" The wooden chair creaked as her mother rocked, the threaded needle moving swiftly in her hand as she sewed a piece of fabric. Her mother's voice was smoke and softness, worn but steady, and it made something in Holera's chest unclench.

Walking past her mother, Holera hung the pot of water on the fire. "Where Exie is concerned, it's always a late night, momma."

Her mother chuckled, the sound warming her heart. With her father being gone, her mother was all she had left. "You never know what to expect with that one. How is she? I know she's had a hard time in the past years..."

Holera lowered herself onto the arm of the settee, the topic of Exie's fallen lover an unexpected one. Her mother hadn't said it explicitly, but it was implied. Exie's former lover, Theoni, the female she thought would be hers forever, had been killed in an explosion at the docks five years earlier. It had nearly broken Exie, leaving her a shell of who she once was. Even now, Exie's laughter carried a sharp edge, as if she had to fight for every scrap of joy.

Holera loosened a breath. "She's Exie. She's strong."

Her mother nodded, the movement seeming to flow with the rocking of her chair. "Stones are strong, wildfire, but they still erode away in the storm. If she doesn't take time to properly grieve, it'll just eat away at her."

Holera swallowed hard. Her mother wasn't just speaking about Exie. The same could be said of her father, of herself.

If anyone knew about grief, it was her mother. Holera touched her mother's hand as she stood, taking the pot from the hearth. "I know that, momma. I'm looking out for her."

It felt like a promise spoken aloud—one Holera already carried like armor.

Chapter Five

HOLERA

All Holera could do when she shifted back into her fae form in the palace courtyard and smoothed out her crisp white tunic was exhale. The marble courtyard gleamed under torchlight, polished too bright for her taste. Everything in the palace smelled faintly of beeswax and formality. She refused to wear a gown, no matter the occasion, but she knew she'd earn at least one raised eyebrow from Otera. If anyone wanted her in silk, they could pry her into it after death. It may have been court, a party in the palace, but she was who she was.

Staring at the enormous wooden doors for a moment, and at the two uniformed males standing on either side, she counted to ten to build her patience. If Exie acted up tonight... Well, she didn't want to think about that. She needed to stay out of trouble, at least for a little while. Tightening the buckle of her sword belt because she was a warrior first, Holera took a step forward, opening the door and entering the foyer.

With the arrival of emissaries, the palace was in full swing, servants bustling around, holding trays and shuffling people to where they needed to go. The air smelled of roasted meats and polished silver. Everywhere she looked, strangers glittered in velvet and gems, their voices a chorus she wanted no part of. Holera ignored all of them, walking briskly toward the eastern wing, the location of the ballroom. She knew the drill. It hadn't been her first time at such an event, although she'd always hoped one would be her last.

Unlike queens in the past, Queen Otera didn't usually bother with such finery, with constant balls and royal events. Otera was a queen who focused on the kingdom's people and running its military and economy. She didn't have time for such distractions, but when visitors from other kingdoms came by—that was when the silver had to be shined and appearances had to be kept up. There were expectations of royalty in Ekotoria, and Otera wasn't one to break that mold, at least not in the face of allies.

Music met Holera's ears before she could even see the golden embossed ballroom doors, and she gritted her teeth. It was not the style of music she preferred, the unrefined quartets of the taverns her preferred style. Instead, stringed instruments fluttered in the air, all plucks and flourishes, so precise it set her teeth on edge. Give her a tavern fiddle out of tune over this any day. The double doors of the ballroom opened, and she had no choice but to enter. It was her punishment, after all.

Although there were dozens of people already in the ballroom when Holera entered, Exie stood out among the crowd. With as tall as she was, as wild as her blond mane was, it would have been nearly impossible for her not to. Exie stood out like a bonfire in a room of candles, mane wild, grin reckless. She turned toward the entrance as soon as Holera walked in, a mischievous smirk on her face, and Holera realized they were already in trouble again. They hadn't done anything yet, but she could feel it. When her friend shot back a glass of whiskey and turned on her heel, making a beeline for her, there was no doubt in her mind. Exie was up to something.

Holera groaned, snatching a glass of the liquid fire from a passing servant's tray and drinking it quickly as Exie swaggered toward her, full of more bravado than one person should ever have. When she finally stopped walking, flicking a nonexistent piece of lint from the collar of her solid black tunic, Holera rolled her eyes. The gesture was so exaggerated it made her want to groan louder than she already had. "What? What are you so uppity about, Ex? I'm not in the mood for any of your shenanigans tonight. I—"

One very long finger pressed against Holera's lips mid sentence, stopping her monologue. "Can you just hush for a second, Holera? I promise to show you what I'm smiling about."

When Exie's finger moved, Holera sighed loudly. "Well? Then spill."

Exie's honey-tinted eyes nearly glowed in the candlelight of the space as she looked over her shoulder, still not sharing the secret she seemed to be keeping. "Have you seen Otera yet?"

Holera followed her line of sight but didn't see the crimson hair of the queen anywhere. People dressed in finery moved about the room, some Aegrician, others with the leathery wings of Norithae, even a few from kingdoms Holera did not recognize, but she didn't see the queen. "No. Exie, I just got here. Obviously I didn't see Otera." Stomping her boot on the ground, the patience she'd been counting on already running out, Holera loosened another breath. "Stop playing games, Ex. Why are you asking if I've seen Otera?"

One of their friends sauntered up, interrupting the conversation. Calista, one of the healers from the Aegrician capital's main infirmary, looked stunning in an emerald ball gown. Roughly the same age as the two warriors, they'd learned how to read from the same tutors when they'd been merely children. "I didn't expect to see the two of you here." She smirked, taking a deep sip of her wine. "Let me guess...punishment?"

Impatience building inside her, Holera reached for another glass of whiskey just as a servant passed them by. There wouldn't be enough alcohol in all of Flamecliff if Calista didn't scurry on and let Exie get on with her story. She wandered away for a moment, allowing the two females to talk amongst themselves.

By the time the burning had settled in Holera's throat from her second glass, and she'd thoroughly scanned the ballroom a second time over, Exie had finished telling of her harrowing ordeal in the tavern the night before, and Calista had walked off. "Well?"

She knew there had been a clip in her voice, but Exie didn't seem to notice. The whiskey seemed to be dulling her senses already, which was always the way her shenanigans started. It seemed to be a common theme in any event in which she got into trouble, and she always seemed to pull Holera down with her.

Exie leaned forward, speaking just into Holera's ear. "The sexy male you met last night...he's meeting with the queen."

Holera nearly choked on her drink. Of course Exie would drop that bomb here, in the middle of the queen's ballroom.

Chapter Six
KASON

Kason's meeting with Queen Otera had been planned for weeks; it was why he'd traveled by ship from the southern part of the continent to be in the city of Flamecliff in time. What he hadn't intended when he'd gone to the Singing Lantern Tavern the night before, a place he'd frequented before becoming a diplomat for the crown, was that he'd have to capture two Warbotach mercenaries who'd followed his mate and her friend out of the tavern. He'd only just met the silver-haired warrior, but it only took one glance into her beautiful violet eyes to know that he was looking into the eyes of his bonded, the female he would make his in all ways... if she didn't kick his ass first. It had certainly happened a time or two before. He just had that effect on females. Chuckling to himself, he took another deep draw of the golden whiskey in his glass and returned to where the queen was standing, her own warrior-female mate guarding her at every step. Kason wasn't sure what the two Warbotach barbarians had in store for his female and her friend, but he had enjoyed beating them to a bloody pulp before they'd been thrown into the dungeon below the palace. It was the queen's decision to determine what to do with them next, although Kason had some ideas.

Queen Otera was the perfect ruler for Aegricia, strong but fair, fierce, and with a mind for governing and commerce. Although the succession as queen has always been chosen by the Aegrician crown as opposed to a royal bloodline, Otera had been fortunate to have lived under her grandmother as queen.

Faenia Lumino, Otera's grandmother, had been queen for nearly one hundred years, but was murdered just before she stepped down to allow the crown to choose someone to take over the throne. It had been a dark time in Aegrician history, when a maliciously ambitious young noblewoman named Joneira Eternus had tried to take the throne by force, calculating the murders of not only Otera's grandmother and mother, but also her sister, Messalina, who was expected to be chosen as the next queen. After losing her entire family in quick succession, no one would have blamed Otera if she'd simply crumbled, walked away from royal life altogether. But she didn't. Instead, the crown chose Otera, and she stood tall, wearing the most powerful crown in their world with unrelenting pride. It was inspiring to her people.

The queen's eyes lit up as Kason approached and set a fresh glass of whiskey in her hand, raising his own for a toast. "To prosperous trade," he said, drinking the rest of the liquid fire in his glass and slamming it down on the table.

"With you handling our trade agreements, Kason, I think we will have nothing but prosperous trade." Not one to fluff up her words, he knew the queen meant exactly what she'd said. He was damn good at his job so it was nice to hear his ruler acknowledge that.

Blaedia caught his eye and he smiled at her, although the general rarely smiled back, at least not when she was in uniform. Come to think of it, he wasn't sure if he'd ever seen the silver-eyed warrior without her uniform on.

When Otera turned to her lover, however, and held out a hand for Blaedia to take it, the general's lips did tip up in the corners, at least for a moment. "Shall we return to the party?" Otera asked, turning her attention back to Kason who nodded as he reached for another glass of whiskey from a server's tray.

Holding his glass in one hand and smoothing his long dark hair that was tied back in a leather strap with the other, Kason followed the queen and her mate out of the private offices and into the ballroom.

The whiskey was strong, which was something Kason was glad for. It would take several glasses of the liquid fire for him to handle the frilly music being played in the ballroom. If it had been up to him, he would've left the party and returned to the tavern, maybe even run into the gorgeous warrior again. He needed to see her again if he was going to make her his mate. Maybe he would be able to sneak away eventually, once Otera was fully engaged with her other guests and no longer paying attention to him.

The entire thought about leaving the party to find his mate flew out of his mind as quickly as a phoenix on the wind when he saw her across the room, the violet eyes of his silver-haired phoenix warrior staring back at him. Her eyes grew wide when she caught sight of him and she took a step forward before stopping herself and grabbing a glass of whiskey from a nearby table.

When she shot the liquid fire back into her mouth in one swig, Kason couldn't help but to chuckle. He'd never wanted a female who wore dresses and acted dainty, who spent their time doing needlework and anything else females typically did in their free time. He still didn't know her name, the female he would one day call his mate, but by the cut of muscles on her arms and shoulders, he could tell she was a fierce warrior, probably an expert with the sword and with a bow. Just thinking about her strong body pulling a bow string taut and shooting an arrow into her enemy made his cock grow hard in his trousers. She was the sexiest thing he'd ever seen, even in her tunic and trousers, but he couldn't wait to see her in fighting leathers. Maybe he could even get her to wear them to his bed. Tired of waiting for her to come to him, Kason swallowed back the last of the contents in his glass and sauntered toward her with a mischievous smirk on his face, her own face mirroring the sentiment.

"If I had to guess, beautiful warrior, I would say you're following me."

Chapter Seven
HOLERA

It was unlike Holera to find herself without words, but when the sexy male from the tavern stepped in front of her, all swagger and confidence, asking if she'd been following him, she couldn't find her tongue. Her mouth opened, but all that came out was silence. Holera hated silence—it made her feel exposed.

Unfortunately, the borderline inebriated Exie had no such reservations, slamming her whiskey glass into his in an overly dramatic cheers. "And I would guess you may be following Holera." She winked at Holera like a mischievous older sister before sauntering away, parting the crowd as she went, leaving chaos in her wake.

The male's face turned to the blond warrior, one eyebrow arched to a point, and grinned. The pure cockiness in his expression only made him sexier. Dipping his chin in Exie's direction, he turned his sights back on Holera, who'd yet to utter a word. "Holera, is it? I'm Kason. Nice to officially meet you."

"I...um...nice to meet you too." Exie's playful hum still lingered in Holera's ears, but when she turned back to Kason, he was watching her. "Sorry about Exie. She's not exactly shy."

Chuckling, he handed her another glass of whiskey. With her nerves where they were, she needed it. "We all have a friend like her. They keep things interesting."

She may have known little about Kason, but he certainly spoke the truth. Taking a deep drink of her whiskey, she willed the liquid fire to calm her nerves. She hated how her hands trembled. Battle she could handle. This? This was worse. Something about this male made her forget how to use her voice.

He seemed to understand this and lifted his arm for her to take. "Shall we find a place to sit and talk, preferably far away from the band?" When he turned to glance over his shoulder, she stifled a giggle and then silently berated herself for acting like a lovesick fledgling. "The music at this party is awful."

Sliding her arm into his, Holera took another sip of her whiskey, the liquid warming her from the inside out. "We can sit in the gardens. The fountains may adequately drown out the music."

The suggestion only broadened the smile on Kason's handsome face, and he dipped his chin, holding out his hand before him, signaling for her to show him the way.

They walked arm-in-arm at a leisurely pace, Holera paying little mind to everyone else at the party. She saw Otera in her peripheral vision, the queen in deep conversation with her mate, but she didn't see Exie again before they'd crossed through the open doorway and out into the back gardens. All she could hope was that her friend stayed out of trouble so she could actually learn a little bit more about the powerful male on her arm, a privilege she had not been afforded the night before.

The night air was brisk, the breeze from the sea leaving the scent of brine on the air. The sharp cold bit her cheeks, carrying salt from the sea. After the heavy perfume of the ballroom, it was a relief. Holera breathed in deeply, the masculine aroma of the male on her arm filling her senses as he led her to one of the several benches facing the sea. With the moon full, its light reflected off the surface of the water, along with the sparkles of a thousand stars. The large fountain at their backs drowned out the sound of the band, as well as the voices of the other partygoers, leaving them in an intimate silence. Kason's arm remained hooked in hers as they sat on the bench, his long legs stretched out before him. They remained quiet for a long moment, the tranquility of the garden too perfect to interrupt.

"I have a confession to make," he said as he turned to face her, his green eyes brilliant in the moonlight.

"You do?" She'd been almost afraid to ask, but she knew he would say whatever he had on his mind anyway. "What is it that you have to confess, Kason?"

Grinning, he drained the rest of his drink and set the empty glass on the ground at his feet. "After last night, I'd hoped to see you again."

It wasn't what Holera had expected him to say, but she wasn't disappointed. Gods help her, she liked the way he said it. After so long without a lover, her heart had chilled with the temperature of her bed, and she yearned to warm it once again. "Is that so?"

Sliding his arm out of hers, Kason took her hand, bringing it to his lips and kissing it. He did it so easily, like she was already precious to him. No one had ever treated her that way before. Her breath caught in her throat as she held his eyes in hers. "It is."

Interlacing his fingers with hers, Kason laid their joined hands on his lap as he gazed out over the water. She couldn't help but to smile to herself as she watched him. It was such a simple gesture but it meant more to her than he realized. She wasn't naive, however. There was no guarantee she'd ever see him again after this night, but just to be touched for that moment was enough. It would have to be.

"I hoped to see you again too."

She'd never admit it aloud—not to him, not even to Exie—but her chest ached with how much she wanted more.

Chapter Eight

KASON

Holera. Her name sounded powerful, yet alluring, which was exactly what the female sitting next to Kason was. It fit her—every syllable steady, unbending, like the warrior she was. He'd meant to tell her about the Warbotach mercenaries, but what good would that do? Better to let her believe the night had been untouched by danger. Better she slept soundly.

Holera stretched her long legs out in front of her, and Kason found it impossible to avoid admiring her figure, her long limbs, muscles finely cut from her life as an Aegrician warrior. She was incredible, but he had a feeling she didn't realize how incredible she truly was. He wanted her to see herself the way he saw her, someone fierce enough to face the world and extraordinary enough to change it.

"You are stunning, Holera." Even among the fae, silver hair and violet eyes were rare. Sitting below the night sky, her hair had the appearance of liquid moonlight as she turned to look at him, her hair sliding over her shoulder.

He expected her to speak, to say something, but she only gazed at him, her free hand twisting into the hem of her cloak. She was nervous, he realized, and he wanted to ease that in her too. Even though he knew little about her, something in her nearness, in her scent, made him want to give her the world, to lay it out at her feet if it would make her his. The porcelain skin of her cheek begged for him to touch it and he didn't want to fight it. Instead, Kason lifted a hesitant hand to her face, searching her eyes for resistance as he cupped her cheek.

Her breath hitched, and the sound faltered in a way that made his chest ache. A tremor moved through her beneath his palm, and he knew his touch had set her alight. She didn't look away. That silence was all the permission he needed.

He leaned in slowly, giving her every chance to turn aside. When his lips finally touched hers, the world dropped away. For a moment she went still, her jaw tight as though she meant to push him away. Kason braced for rejection, but then her shoulders eased, her lips softened against his, and the heat of her answer surged into him. Whatever protest she had died unspoken, and he knew then she wanted this as much as he did. The first kiss was fleeting, a spark testing dry tinder. The second burned deeper, certainty replacing caution, and the warmth of her mouth consumed him.

The fire inside him roared, rising higher with every beat of his heart. Her mouth moved against his with an urgency that caught him off guard, and the sound of it—the soft catch of her breath between kisses—nearly undid him. He tasted whiskey and salt, but beneath it was something wholly her own, something that already felt like addiction.

What had begun tentative became hungry. His control slipped with every stroke of her lips, every answering push of her tongue. She wasn't simply returning the kiss; she was claiming him as surely as he longed to claim her, and the thought sent heat flooding his body until nothing mattered but holding her closer, kissing her harder, and never letting her go.

Although her conversations had been reserved, shy even, ever since they'd met, her kisses were not. When Kason wrapped his arms around her body, pulling her in close, she climbed onto his lap, straddling him as they sat on the bench by the sea. The wind whipped at her hair, sliding under her cloak and making her shiver, giving Kason permission to hold her tighter, to wrap her up in his cloak and against his body while their mouths explored one another, while their tongues tasted. Caressed.

With as hard as she'd made it, he knew Holera could feel his cock pressing against the fabric of his trousers. It didn't give her pause. If anything, it fueled her as she wrapped her legs around the sides of him and ground against his hardness, the friction pulling a breathy moan from her mouth. The sound threatened to make him come undone, but he didn't want to rush things with her. She wasn't just some female at a brothel, or a night of release with a stranger at a tavern. Holera would be his forever, so he wanted to take his time with her. He wanted to do things right.

When she pulled her lips away from Kason's, he was left panting but wanting more, and she knew it. With a seductive smile, she leaned forward and ran her tongue up the curve of his neck, licking and sucking her way up to his ear. He groaned, his hips bucking up against her in spite of himself. "Are you trying to make me lose control, Holera?"

Huffing a laugh, she returned to his mouth, kissing him hungrily as his arms slid around her waist and gripped her backside.

"Maybe you need to lose control." After being as shy as she'd been the entire night, those were the last words he'd expected to hear from her, and he felt the sultry tone in which she said them all the way down his shaft. If she wanted him to lose control, she wouldn't have to try very hard.

Holera's fingers slid into his hair, removing the leather strap, allowing his long locks to fall free against his back, before returning her attention to his neck. A growl rose from deep in his belly, and resisting taking her right there on that bench was taking more willpower than he'd even thought he had. She ground against him again, the warm friction from between her thighs nearly making him release in his trousers.

"Is there somewhere we can go?" she asked, her voice no more than breath against his ear. A surge of excitement filled him, even if he didn't intend to claim her that night. He still wanted to wait, but he wasn't opposed to finding somewhere they could be alone together.

Nodding, he stood, lifting her with him before gently setting her back onto her own feet. If they were going to walk around where there were others, he didn't think it would've been appropriate for her to still be straddling his waist. Placing his hand on the small of her back, Kason led Holera through the gardens and toward the gate. "I have a room nearby."

CHAPTER NINE

HOLERA

Holera had never considered herself to be one to succumb to passions over having good sense, but there was something about Kason that made all her methodical planning flee from her mind like it was running from an enemy. Her head told her this was reckless, but her body didn't care. For once, she let it win. Just the scent of him, and the feeling of his fingers interlaced with hers, had her straddling his lap and sucking on his neck. She didn't know what had come over her, but she wasn't strong enough to fight it. She wasn't even sure if she wanted to. If only for a moment, she wanted to let her heart lead her and not her head. Fate, it seemed, had other plans.

Just as they were making their way toward the back gates of the palace, intent on finding somewhere more private to spend time together, a clean cut Aegrician male with golden hair and deep umber eyes stepped out into their path.

"Kason. Sorry to interrupt your evening, but there's a situation the queen needs you to attend to."

Kason stiffened at her side, and she fought back a disappointed groan. The words slammed into her like cold water, and she wanted to bare her teeth at him for daring to steal the moment. She didn't even know what he did for the kingdom, or what kind of situation the male was talking about, but she knew her fling, at least for the night, was over. When he turned to face her, the fire in his eyes dimming with an exhale, she knew it was over.

"Wait for me," he said, the words crushing her somewhere deep inside her chest. She hated the way her chest ached, as though she'd let herself hope for more.

All she could do was nod as he gave her one more kiss and his hand slipped out of hers before he disappeared through the open doorway and into the crowd. She stood there for a moment, watching the space where he'd passed refill with revelers, before taking a step inside. Something was going on, and she knew he'd told her to wait for him, but she wasn't the sit-and-wait type. If she was going to get herself in trouble, however, she would need a partner in crime, so instead of going after him, she headed for the bar. First, she needed to find Exie. Thankfully, her friend was right where she'd expected her to be.

Seeming to have sensed Holera approaching, Exie spun around to face her. "There you are! I thought you'd gone home."

The queen catching Holera's eye, she watched as Otera spoke discreetly to one of her guards before leaving the room, Blaedia at her heel. "There's no time to talk about where I've been, Ex. Something's going on and I need to figure out what."

The mischievous sparkle in Exie's eyes nearly made Holera regret going for her friend instead of following Kason. Trouble lit her faster than whiskey ever could. After only a moment, it passed. "Something with Kason?" Draining a glass of water, Exie turned toward the direction in which Otera had gone. "I saw him go that way just before Otera left with Blaedia."

It wasn't their place to get involved in emissary business. Holera knew that, but it didn't sway her. Blowing out a breath, she headed toward the door that would lead them back into the palace corridor, Exie following her lead. If her queen was involved, then she would make it her business.

Walking past the guards posted at the doors, Holera merely nodded once in their direction, hoping her brisk pace would convince them she had urgent business that was not to be interrupted. She hadn't expected them to let her pass, but they did. With no indication of what direction Kason and the queen had gone, aside from the faintest imprint of his scent, she turned left toward the lower levels of the palace. There wasn't much down there aside from the dungeons, but she hadn't mistaken Kason's scent, or Otera's, so she knew that was the way they'd gone.

"What happened between the two of you?" Exie asked as they walked briskly down the corridor leading to the back stairwell. Aside from the guards at the doors, they hadn't passed anyone else.

"We can talk about that later." Stopping at the end of the hall, Holera peered around the corner and down the darkened stairway. With only a few sconces on the wall, most of the space was in shadow. The torches hissed, shadows leaping across stone walls, the air damp and cold enough to raise gooseflesh. "Someone came to get him from the courtyard. Said there was a situation he needed to take care of." Taking one more look over her shoulder, she stepped into the stairwell. "They came this way, Kason and Otera, with a few others."

Lifting her finger to her mouth, Exie silenced any further questions as they began to move down the stone stairs into the subterranean level of the palace. The silence stretched too long, broken only by the echo of their boots. Each step felt heavier than the last. When they arrived at the bottom of the stairs, where a heavy wooden door separated them from the dungeon, the sound of a scream nearly brought Holera to her knees.

Chapter Ten
Kason

Kason knew why he'd been summoned before he even walked into the ballroom. There had been trouble with the Warbotach prisoners, and since he'd brought them in, he knew they were his problem. Although there had been about a dozen Warbotach traders at the tavern the night before, only two of them had been stupid enough to follow Holera and Exie when they'd left the bar, therefore there were only two of them in the dungeon below the palace. At least, that's how many there had been when he'd last seen them. The problem was, once he arrived back in the dungeon after the queen summoned him, there had been only one prisoner remaining. Somehow, one of the bastards had escaped.

Kason growled under his breath. He'd found the female he'd been dreaming about, one he'd surely settle down for, but he had been forced to leave her standing in the courtyard with no explanation. Once he finished interrogating the remaining prisoner, he would have to find Holera and beg for her forgiveness. If he could even find her. Panos' interruption as they were making their way off the palace grounds had drowned their fire like a bucket of cold water.

Otera, Blaedia, and two guards entered the dungeon behind Kason, the prisoner already tied to a chair. Torchlight guttered along damp stone, the air thick with mildew and the iron tang of blood.

"How'd this happen?" he asked no one in particular. The prisoner struggled against his bindings, spewing curses in his own language. Kason understood every word but refused to dignify the filth with a translation.

"Seems the other prisoner overpowered our guard, left through the servant's entrance." Taking a cursory glance at the unconscious guard leaning against the stone wall, Kason cracked his knuckles. It appeared as though he wouldn't be returning to his female anytime soon. The thought made his jaw tighten. Every wasted moment here was one stolen from her.

Otera moved further into the room, Blaedia at her side. "Has anyone gone after the prisoner? We need him captured before he gets on a ship. Needless to say, Warbotach would see his imprisonment as an act of war."

The male guard nodded, his body language showing signs of his frayed nerves. "I sent out six guards, Your Majesty. Four on foot and two in the sky."

"How long ago?" Kason demanded, still not understanding why there had only been one guard watching the prisoners to begin with. It was an oversight that wouldn't happen again.

"An hour, maybe less."

With the unsure tone of the guard's voice, Kason was betting it was less. He gritted his teeth. "Send out more." With a swift nod, the guard left the room and headed back into the palace proper.

Otera turned to her lover, squeezing Blaedia's hand. "Go. Send your own trusted warriors after him. We have to get that prisoner back."

Blaedia nodded, but just as she turned toward the heavy wooden door leading out of the dungeon, there were two figures standing in the doorway. "Holera. Exie. What are you two doing here?" Her voice cracked like a whip in the stale air, and the weight of her glare could have crushed stone. The general sounded less than pleased, but both females had the appearance of someone caught in a trap. They knew they had been found somewhere they shouldn't have been.

Holera's mouth opened and shut a few times like a fish out of water before she finally spoke. "I—I heard a scream. I thought someone was hurt."

Mouth twisting in a smirk, Kason knew Holera was lying. She'd heard a scream, but not until she was already in the dungeon, exactly where she shouldn't have been. Eyes like slits, Blaedia glared at her two warriors for a few awkward moments before seeming to realize they were not in the right frame of mind to go after a barbarian, Exie being slightly intoxicated and Holera too distracted by the male across the room to be given orders. With one more glance over her shoulder, Blaedia left the dungeon.

Once her general was out of the way, Holera stepped further into the room, confusion clear on her face as she took in the space. "What is this, Kason? What's going on?"

Kason hadn't intended to disclose the truth about how he'd followed them home the night before because they were being trailed by barbarians who'd intended on doing them harm. He'd hoped to leave that storyline out of their night together, but he no longer had the choice as the beautiful warrior glanced from the Warbotach prisoner tied to the chair, and back to the male she'd just been kissing in the gardens.

With nothing else for her to do, the queen left the room, leaving two guards behind to watch over the remaining prisoner. Still, Kason didn't feel comfortable walking away just yet. Instead, he dragged the bound male back into his cell, double checking the lock once he closed the door. He needed the prisoner secured before he could even think of touching her again. Only then did he allow himself the indulgence of reaching for her hand. Taking Holera by the hand, he pulled her to him and kissed her deeply, relieved when she fell into him instead of pulling away.

"Come, let's take a seat just outside and I'll explain everything."

Chapter Eleven

Holera

Holera's mind whirled as she'd glanced from Kason, to the queen, to the prisoner tied to a metal chair in the dungeon. She was relieved the scream hadn't come from her newly found lover, but she recognized the Warbotach brute in the chair. He'd been the same male Exie had had an altercation with the night before, and she didn't know why he'd been captured. As she walked hand in hand with Kason through the servant's exit and out into the crisp night air, Exie remained behind to give them privacy. Kason walked her to one of the stone benches, dropping to sit beside her.

"I haven't been completely forthcoming with you tonight," he said, the words sending Holera's heart into her gut. "After you left the tavern with Exie last night, two of the Warbotach merchants followed you."

The words struck her harder than any blade, leaving her stomach hollow. Knowing she'd been followed by two males didn't ease the sinking in her stomach. Holera shook her head, disappointed in herself for having been so distracted by Exie that she hadn't even realized they'd been in danger. "I can't believe I didn't know. I was so caught up with—"

"Don't." Kason cut her off, sliding his hand to the nape of her neck and rubbing the flesh between her shoulders. His voice was steady, a warmth meant to anchor her even in the cold night air. "Don't blame yourself for what they did, or what they tried to do. I have no doubt that, if they had attacked, you would have been able to defend yourself. What matters is that you didn't have to. I saw them through the windows of the tavern, and I cut them off before they could do whatever it was they intended to do."

Just thinking about what those merchants had planned for her and her friend made bile rise in Holera's throat. "Thank you for protecting us." In all her life, she had never seen herself as needing anyone's protection, but in that moment, she felt helpless, and she hated it.

Kason pulled her closer, wrapping his arm around her waist. "But one of those bastards got away—about an hour ago. They've sent out more guards to look for him, but I need to look for him as well. We can't let him get on a ship. I just didn't want to leave without seeing you. I didn't want you to think I'd run away from you."

"I want to go with you."

Although she expected Kason to deny her request, he didn't. Instead, he rose from the bench, reaching a hand down to help her up before pulling her into a kiss. For just a moment, the world around them disappeared as Kason's scent filled her senses, and his tongue caressed her own. The kiss was brief but consuming, a promise more than a surrender, and it left her aching when he broke away.

When they parted, it took every bit of her restraint not to drag him back to her lips again, but they had to find the missing prisoner. She didn't need Kason to explain what would be the fallout if the Warbotach merchant got on a ship and returned to his own kingdom with claims of being imprisoned by the Aegrician monarch. Lesser grievances had started wars in their world.

Returning to the dungeon, Holera filled Exie in on what had happened the night before, how her near bar brawl had gotten them followed, had nearly gotten them into more trouble than they could have even imagined. Kason saw to the remaining prisoner while Exie and Holera talked, ensuring he was not only secure in his cell, but that there were enough guards watching him to prevent him from escaping. If Exie's argument in the tavern had started a war... That was something Holera couldn't even think about at the moment, but she could tell by the look on her friend's face that Exie felt some moniker of regret for her temper, even if she'd been defending their queen. Her shoulders slumped in a way Holera rarely saw, her bravado cracked by the weight of what might have been.

They left the dungeon a moment later. Kason held onto Holera, with Exie on their heels, as they climbed the stairs out of the lower levels and back into the palace proper. There were many warriors now guarding the lower levels of the palace, including the doors into the ballroom. Bypassing the party area altogether, the trio left through the front doors and stepped out into the cool night air.

"We should fly," Exie said, coming to a stop in front of them. "With Kason on your back, we'll have more eyes in the sky. We'll find him."

Kason nodded, securing his weapons on his back. Holera hadn't had many people on her back, but she knew it could give them a better chance. In a flash of fire, she shifted, a brilliant silver phoenix standing where she had been. Her feathers shimmered under the moonlight, heat rippling the air as sparks skittered across the stones. Wasting no time, Kason climbed onto her back and shifted his weight until he was nestled and out of the way of her wings.

Pulling reins out of her satchel, Exie secured them onto her friend, passing the handholds to Kason before shifting into her own phoenix form. Where Holera's phoenix form was silver with a flare of violet feathers on her tail and wings, Exie was a brilliant fire red, with tail feathers of every color of the rainbow, and a tuft of blond feathers on her head. Even in that shape, Exie radiated chaos, her wings slicing the air with reckless power.

The two phoenixes nodded to each other and then spread their wings, their tails fluttering in the wind as they lifted into the sky, eyes searching for their prey.

Chapter Twelve
KASON

In all his decades of life, Kason had never ridden on the back of a phoenix warrior, so he was hesitant to climb onto Holera. The birds were massive, but so was he, and he didn't want to hurt her. Her feathers radiated heat, the air around her shimmering faintly with phoenix fire. Ultimately, however, Exie's words made sense, and he knew Holera was more than capable of carrying his weight, even if he always saw himself as carrying his female, and not the other way around. Thinking of her as his brought warmth to his chest, even in the cold night. A mate was something he'd never imagined for himself. Truly bonding to a mate, having fate know exactly who was meant for a person, was rare.

Soaring through the air, firmly positioned behind the phoenix's neck, Kason pulled his bow from over his shoulder, notching an arrow and peering into the darkness. With Exie in the lead, they flew low over the city streets and toward the harbor. Below them, lanterns glimmered in crooked rows, the alleys alive with faint shouts and torchlight.

In the darkness, even with his advanced fae eyesight and the even more impressive eyesight of the phoenixes, it would still be difficult to find the escaped prisoner. The number of merchants and ships in the harbor would only make the search that much harder. He could have hidden in plain sight from them among the crowds and gotten on a ship before he'd ever been found.

Blowing out a breath, Kason leaned forward, stroking Holera's silky feathers as he leaned into the wind. Her avian face was severe, every line marked with danger, yet to him she was still beautiful, extraordinary. He knew what she could do, what all the phoenix warriors could do. Her talons were the size of his fingers, and her razor-sharp beak was a weapon. She could rip a man apart in her phoenix form, but she was no less fierce in her fae form. When they were back on the ground and had time to spend together, he wanted to spar with her, wanted to see her slick with sweat and wielding a sword. He couldn't imagine anything sexier than Holera in fighting leathers, swinging a weapon, and kicking his ass. The thought alone had his blood surging with more force than the wind on his face.

The memory of her straddling his lap, grinding against his hardness, pulsed through him with every wingbeat. Her scent in his nose and the taste of her skin against his lips had nearly driven him over the edge, and his body yearned to have her on top of him again. If they found the missing prisoner, Kason hoped he and Holera could return to the night they were heading toward. A night of passion and getting to know each other better so he could convince her that he was meant to be her mate. The more time he spent with her, the more he needed her.

His cock already firming in his trousers, Kason shook the thoughts from his mind and returned his eyes to scan the harbor below. The Warbotach ship still bobbed against the docks, merchants loading cargo on and off the craft while others completed the last of their tasks in the city. The masts rocked like skeletal fingers against the night sky, ropes creaking under the weight of crates. Just as he scanned the barbarians who were loading crates across the ramp, he laid eyes on the male who'd gotten away.

"There!"

Both birds' eyes darted in the direction of Kason's outstretched hand, their eyes locking on their target. Exie dove first, her vibrant wings whipping out at her sides to aim her decline as her brilliant tail ribbons fluttered behind her, coloring the sky like a rainbow in the darkness. Following her friend, Holera's strong body shot like an arrow at the Warbotach vessel, her massive silver wings tilting to control their descent. Kason held onto her back with his thighs, his bow held high with the arrow pulled taut as he pinned his eyes on the escaped prisoner. If the male got away, war would return to Aegricia's shores, and that was something they needed to prevent.

The other guards and warriors approached from multiple directions, some flying in over the sea, and others through the forest, or from the road. They were all closing in on the Warbotach ship. The entire situation was precarious. If Aegricia forced their way onto a Warbotach vessel and took one of their people, even that could be seen as an act of war, so there were no perfect options on how to deal with the situation.

Exie swooped past them, a keening call erupting from her beak as she signaled the other winged warriors to follow her into the forest and out of sight of the Warbotach ship. Holera followed as Kason gestured to the soldiers on the ground to watch but wait. They knew where the prisoner was. Now they needed to figure out the best way to apprehend him without drawing too much attention.

Chapter Thirteen
Holera

Following Exie into the forest, Holera landed in a clearing next to her friend and allowed Kason to climb off her back before shifting back into her fae body. The clearing smelled of damp earth and pine, the forest pressing in close as though listening. Although she could communicate with the other phoenixes in her phoenix form, she could not speak that way, and they needed to discuss what to do next.

"His men know he's back on board," Kason said, sliding his bow over his shoulder. "There won't be any way for us to detain him without alerting his friends."

Exie kicked at the dirt, her boot striking hard enough to scatter pebbles, her restless energy a storm barely contained. "So, either we let him go or get into a fight with the entire ship of Warbotach merchants? Is that what you're telling me?"

It was a scenario Holera had been afraid of. Their kingdom didn't want to go to war, no matter what the Warbotach soldiers had been intending. "So, what do we do? Do we just let him go? The risk of there being a battle if we enter their ship is too high."

"Unless..." The tone of Exie's voice was enough to make Holera clench her teeth because it was one that usually came before an idea that would get them both into trouble.

"I want no part in your schemes, Exie. I already got into enough trouble with Blaedia today. My legs are still sore from chasing arrows all over the mountain and one of those fledglings nearly took my ear off. You can shove whatever mad plan you're brewing right back into that reckless skull."

Kason chuckled, but didn't disrupt Holera's diatribe until it was over. "I hope this doesn't make you angry with me, my fierce warrior, but I'd like to hear her ideas, even if they're crazy enough to get us into trouble." His grin made it impossible for Holera to stay angry, though she tried.

The smirk that grew on Exie's face only made Holera cringe more, but she didn't object again as her friend laid out her plan.

The plan was foolish to say the least, but Holera went along with it against her better judgment, mostly because she had been overruled. Although infiltrating the Warbotach ship would be asking for a fight, that was exactly what they planned to do.

Under the cover of darkness and swooping in from the water, Kason and Exie intended to sneak onto the Warbotach ship and recapture the prisoner. There were about a million things that could have gone wrong with the plan, including getting themselves captured or killed, but Otera had made it clear they needed to prevent the prisoner from leaving Aegricia, so they didn't see any other options.

Kason kissed her before he left on her friend's back, and it had taken nearly everything in Holera to let them go. She was a warrior, so she knew the risks associated with her station in life, but it didn't make it any easier when doing something that put herself or those she cared about in danger.

While Exie and Kason took to the skies and out over the water, Holera snuck through the dense forest toward the harbor. Exie intended to drop Kason on the stern and then return once he had the prisoner in hand. While Exie circled overhead and Kason snuck onto the ship to find their target, Holera was to be the lookout.

She waited near the bank, the brush of the forest's edge and bustle of the port keeping her well hidden, and watched as her friends disappeared into the darkened sky. Salt wind stung her nose, carrying the creak of rigging and the muffled shouts of sailors. Every sound set her on edge. Time seemed to stand still as she listened for the sounds of yelling, or the clanging of swords, but for many long moments, there was only the sound of merchants and travelers moving around the city. Her grip tightened on her sword hilt, her pulse thudding in her ears as the quiet stretched too long. Just when she was warring with herself over whether she should go after them, the first sign of trouble erupted from the water's edge.

Chapter Fourteen

KASON

Kason had known Exie's plan was a long shot from the beginning, but they'd had no other choice if they wanted to take the escaped prisoner back into custody before he fled Aegricia. When Exie had first swooped low over the water, allowing Kason to leap onto the poop deck, he'd done so without being seen. With his dagger in hand, he crept across onto the quarterdeck, his dark hooded cloak disguising his face, and slipped into the galley. The ship creaked around him, the stink of stale ale and sweat hanging thick in the air.

He'd found his target quicker than he'd expected. Seeming to feel confident he was as good as free, the male they'd been looking for was lounging just below deck, a tankard of ale dripping down his wrist, his grin smug with false freedom. Holding his dagger at the Warbotach male's side, Kason had escorted the prisoner back to where Exie had left him only a few minutes before. The problem was, although he'd snuck onto the ship without being seen, his dagger hadn't been enough of a deterrent, and the male in his hold put up a fight once Exie had appeared in the distance.

Kason tried to neutralize the issue, slamming his fist into the male's jaw as his dagger clattered to the planks, the sound sharp as a bell in the chaos. But Warbotach males were raised to fight, and the strike hadn't so much as phased the prisoner. Before he knew it, Exie had landed on the deck, shifting into her fae form, and three more Warbotach males had joined them for a full-on brawl.

Ducking a swinging sword, Kason drew his own from its scabbard and pivoted to face two of their attackers. Exie, wielding a blade of her own, slashed at one of the males, hitting him in the arm. Blood sprayed across the deck, slicking the boards beneath their boots.

"Cunt!" he barked out, the wound gushing as he swung his other arm out, his machete narrowly missing the side of her face.

Exie barked a laugh even as she swung her blade. "You wish you got some!"

From what he'd seen of her, Exie had no fear—not in a tavern, and not here—and somehow that reckless spark made Kason grin even as steel whistled around him.

He pulled his other sword from over his back, slicing both through the air. Although he missed one of his opponents, the male jumping back to avoid the blow, one of his blades caught the escaped prisoner across the chest. Without the magic of a healer, the wound had the potential to kill him, and he seemed to realize that. Stumbling to the railing of the deck, the prisoner dropped, his arm wrapping across his chest as the male who'd been fighting Kason ran for help.

Taking advantage of the distraction, Kason reached for Exie, yanking her by the top of her leathers toward the railing. "We need to get out of here. Now!"

Nodding, she shifted in a burst of brilliant flame. Tossing the injured prisoner over his shoulder, Kason jumped onto the phoenix's back right before her wings launched them into the air and over the water.

Just as Exie soared closer to the land, an enormous silver figure surged toward them. Holera approached, her massive phoenix wings carrying her alongside them as they flew against the chilly wind. Although he'd asked her to remain in the forest as a lookout, mostly because he'd wanted to keep her safe, she'd completely ignored him when she'd heard the fight break out, and it only sharpened his hunger for her. She was reckless, yes, but gods, she was glorious. She would be just as fierce of a mate, loving when she needed to love, and fighting when she needed to fight. Even though he couldn't communicate with her in that form, Kason winked at the beautiful warrior, her severe violet eyes flaring before both birds turned, aiming toward the palace just as the sun began to rise.

Chapter Fifteen
Holera

By the time they'd landed back on the palace grounds with the escaped Warbotach prisoner, Holera was exhausted and more than a little frustrated with what had come to pass. She hadn't slept, and the night's chaos pressed down on her like lead. They'd retrieved the Warbotach male, but nothing else had gone as planned. She hadn't been on the ship when Exie and Kason had grabbed him, but she'd heard the commotion from the forest. Whatever happened on that ship, the rest of the Warbotach merchants probably knew about it. She didn't even want to imagine what the fallout would be once they returned to their home country and reported the attack. Even though two of their merchants started the whole mess by following her and Exie, that didn't mean the barbarian king would see it in the same way, nor did that mean he would see the attack on their ship as having been warranted. She was grateful Kason and Exie were unharmed, but that was about all she was grateful for at that moment.

Shifting back into her fae form next to Exie and Kason, Holera reached to help Kason with the prisoner, who was bleeding profusely from a chest wound, as her friend shifted. Blood slicked her fingers as she steadied him with Kason, the stench of iron sharp in her nose.

"He needs a healer quickly or he's not going to make it," Kason said, the prisoner's head lolling to the side as he fought for consciousness. Exie nodded, darting toward the palace and disappearing through the doors.

"What happened?" Each taking on some of the injured male's weight, Kason and Holera staggered toward the infirmary inside the palace after Exie.

"Everything went to shit when I tried to get him off the ship. The bastard started fighting and his friends joined in. Exie and I had to fight off a few before we were able to leave."

Holera's jaw tightened, her teeth grinding as she wrestled her frustration down. "I knew it was a bad idea from the start. Now the entire ship of merchants is going to go back to Warbotach and their king will wage an attack."

Just as they were about to attempt to open the palace doors with limited free hands, several guards came out with a board and they were able to set the injured male on it to relieve themselves of the burden. The guards disappeared into the corridor with the prisoner, leaving Kason and Holera on the foyer, both of them drenched in blood.

"I still have a place nearby, if you want to get cleaned up. I have a room at the inn above the Singing Lantern."

Holera watched his face for a minute, the male incredibly rugged and sexy, and debated if she wanted to pick up where they'd left off in the courtyard. There were many bathing rooms in the palace they could use if they wanted to, but after everything they'd gone through in just over twenty-four hours, she didn't know if she was ready for everyone in the palace to know about their budding romance just yet. She also couldn't get their encounter in the gardens out of her mind, even with the events that had occurred since.

Looking down at her hands again, sticky with the blood of her enemy, she made her decision. The gore on her skin was jarring against the thought of his kiss in the gardens, both fresh in her mind, both impossible to ignore. "Yeah. Let's get out of here. As long as the queen knows where to find you if we're needed. Exie can just assume I went home to clean up and rest. I can do without her getting me into trouble for a while. I may need to borrow clothes though...even if they're way too large for me."

Kason chuckled, touching a bloody hand to the small of her back and leading her toward the palace gates. His chuckle was low, the touch at her back both steadying and possessive. "I'm sure we can manage to find you something."

Chapter Sixteen
Kason

With his hand against Holera's back, Kason led her toward the palace gates and onto the street. He realized the fallout of their fight on the Warbotach ship could end up causing a bigger conflict, but he and Holera needed to step away from the situation for a while, at least long enough to eat, bathe, and sleep. Many guards and warriors would be sent to monitor the activity in the city and harbor, and others would be used to watch over the injured prisoner, but what the Warbotach male really needed at that moment was a healer, and neither him nor Holera were healers.

Even with the smell of blood and sweat on her skin, the beautiful warrior's scent filled his senses, reminding Kason of the moments they'd shared in the gardens. Although he wanted her more than he'd ever wanted anyone, he had no expectations of moving any farther with her than what she was comfortable with. If she chose him as her mate, they had forever to be together. Holera was worth waiting for.

The sky threatened snow as they made their way down one of the alleys behind the buildings on the main street, not wanting to cause a scene with their gory appearances. Their boots left faint red smears on the cobblestones, reminders of a night that was far from finished. They slipped into the back door of the tavern where they'd first met.

"I'll talk to the barkeep before we go to the room and ask for food and drinks to be brought to us."

Holera nodded, remaining near the stairs as Kason crossed the room and approached the bar. Butterflies filled her belly for the first time in a long time, the feeling unsettling her more than battle ever had. Since she'd been younger and had a male who'd meant something to her, she hadn't felt this way. He hadn't turned out to be the male she wanted to spend her life with, and she'd moved on.

Watching the way the barkeep, an elderly male with graying hair, smiled as he spoke to Kason squeezed her heart. The old man's easy trust in him only deepened the warmth Holera felt watching Kason in his element. Even with his rugged exterior, Kason was kind, personable, someone people naturally liked, except when he had a blade to their throats. He may have been skilled with diplomacy, but he was a trained warrior.

After a brief conversation at the bar, Kason walked back toward her with a grin on his face and a decanter in his hand. "My good friend, Spyro, will be sending up two breakfast plates in a bit, and his mate has plenty of clothing to spare. Actually, he seemed glad to get rid of some of it. He said her things take up the entire cabinet."

Smirking and shaking her head, Holera followed Kason as he led her up the darkened stairway and onto the second level of the building. They walked past several guest rooms down the long corridor, the boards creaking under their weight, lanterns flickering shadows along the narrow hall, before he used a key to unlock the door of the last room on the right, opening it so she could enter first.

"I never did ask you where you live," she said, hesitating for only a moment. Having only known each other for a day, she didn't want to pry. "Since you're staying at the inn, I assume you don't live in the capital?"

Kason closed the door behind him, setting the key and decanter on the table before dropping his weapons to the floor. Holera did the same. "I travel a lot as an emissary for the kingdom, so I don't see my home much, but I do have a cabin in the mountains north of the capital."

Dropping to his knees, he started to unlace her boots. The simple act made her chest tighten; a warrior of his stature humbling himself at her feet was something she'd never imagined. "Can I run a bath for you, my beautiful warrior? We both could use one before we touch any of the furniture in here. I don't want Spyro to demand my head if we destroy anything."

Holera lowered herself into a chair, kicking her boots off as he finished loosening them for her. "That's the best idea I've heard all day."

Chapter Seventeen

HOLERA

Steam circled in tendrils through the air above the tub as Kason ran Holera's bath. The warmth fogged the glass panes and wrapped the room in a cocoon, shutting out the world beyond the door. She watched him for a moment as he leaned over the tub, in awe of how such a rugged male would get on his knees for her, especially when they'd only just met. Although she'd had lovers before, she'd never felt the pull of a mating bond, but she couldn't deny the attraction her body had to Kason. Her body wanted him on a level she would have had a hard time fighting, not that she wanted to fight it at all.

Pulling on the laces of her tunic, Holera loosened the bloody garment enough for it to slide to the floor. As soon as her chest was bare, the chilled air of the room perked her nipples, and Kason turned to look at her, a mischievous look on his face. The heat of the bath beckoned, but the way Kason's gaze swept over her was hotter still. He licked his lips, rising onto his muscular legs and closing the distance between them.

"You are stunning, my fierce warrior." The depth of his voice sent shivers racing across her body. It wasn't just desire in his voice—it was reverence, and that undid her more than lust could have.

Reaching toward him, Holera untied the laces on Kason's tunic and tossed it to the floor, the filthy garment landing just beside hers. The sight of his bare tattooed chest and the rippled muscles of his stomach turned her mouth to sandpaper. She licked her lips, sliding her hands up his chest and around his neck. "You aren't so bad yourself."

Chuckling, he leaned forward and nuzzled into her neck, his mouth against her skin turning her molten. "When this is settled with the Warbotach prisoner, I'd like to take you back to my cabin for a visit—if you'd like to join me."

Nodding, she pulled away to look into his enchanting green eyes. "I'd like that a lot."

Holera reached to unfasten his trousers, but he placed his hand on top of hers, stopping her. "Let's get you a bath first. I'll clean up after."

He watched her eyes as he traced strong fingers from her collarbone, down to her stomach, resting them on the buckle to her trousers. Hesitating for a moment, there was a question in his eyes, a need for permission before going any further. Slipping her hand between them, she unclasped her buckle and pulled him into a kiss as her trousers hit the ground at her feet. Before she'd had a chance to react, Kason scooped her up in his arms and set her down in the deliciously warm water.

Instead of getting in the tub behind her, since it wouldn't have been big enough for the two of them anyway, Kason pulled a stool behind her head and sat down. "Do you want me to wash your hair?"

Although she'd never had another person bathe her, aside from her mother when she was a child, she nodded, closing her eyes as she leaned back. Scooping up water with a cup, Kason poured it slowly over her hair and shoulders, the sensation of the warm water cascading down her body relaxing her nearly to the point of putting her to sleep. She groaned as the scent of lavender hit her nose, the fragrance clinging to the steam, blending with the warmth of his touch until she melted beneath his hands. His deft fingers massaged it into her scalp.

"You shouldn't spoil me like this. I'm going to have a hard time settling for washing my own hair after this."

Kason chuckled and leaned over to kiss her on the shoulder. "I'll spoil you as long as you let me."

Cracking her eyes open, she turned around to face him. "That's quite a commitment."

The look in his eyes was genuine, cherishing even. "It is a commitment, but it's a commitment I want to make to you if you'll have me as your mate." The words, spoken so simply, carried more weight than any vow she had ever heard.

Chapter Eighteen

KASON

Sliding her damp hand around his neck, Holera pulled his lips to hers, kissing him deeper than she ever had before. When she pulled away, Kason was halfway in the bathtub with her, the arms of his tunic soaked. He chuckled, straightening as he peeled off the damp garment and tossed it to the floor. Standing in the tub, Holera's damp silver hair rested over her full breasts as water cascaded over her curves. Droplets tracked down the slope of her stomach, glinting in the candlelight. Just looking at her turned Kason's mouth to sandpaper, stiffening his cock until it pressed uncomfortably against the seam of his trousers. He stepped forward, grabbing the towel from the side of the tub and wrapping it around her body before lifting her and carrying her into the bedchamber. The towel clung to her damp skin, heat radiating through the fabric and straight into his hands.

"Do you want me to set you on the floor or the bed?"

Leaning forward, Holera nuzzled into his neck. "The bed."

Her voice was nothing more than a purr against his skin and he took no more convincing, taking the last few steps to the bed and setting her down, hesitating only a moment before climbing onto the bed next to her.

"Are you sure you want to be my mate, Kason? Even with how little we know each other?" Her voice carried both steel and hesitation, the kind of question only someone who had lost too much before would ask.

Cupping her cheek with his hand, he kissed her, lingering as her scent filled his nose. "I've never been surer about anything. I knew the moment we first touched when we were in the courtyard. I knew I would give you anything."

Her violet eyes watched him for a moment before she spoke and he waited, not wanting to rush her decision. No matter what she decided, he would respect it. "What about your travels? Will I ever see you?"

He chuckled. If that was her biggest concern, it would be an easy fix. "After decades as an Aegrician emissary, I'm tired of always being on the road or on a ship. If I could trade that life for one with you as my companion and my lover, I would make that trade without thought. It's not even a question."

Sliding her hand up his chest and around his back, she pulled him on top of her, Kason settling his hips between her thighs. He'd thought they would take things slower, but if she was ready for more, he had no intention of denying her or himself. She was perfect, and she was under him. He would have been a fool to turn her away.

"We definitely need time to learn more about each other," she said, pulling him into another kiss.

When she licked the seam of his lips, the groan that left him was full of need. The taste of her was intoxicating. Opening for her, his mind got lost in the slide of her tongue against his, of the warmth of the apex of her thighs against the bulge in his trousers. The garment was maddening, but he didn't dare remove that final barrier between their bodies, not until she asked him to. Every muscle in his body screamed to tear the fabric away, but her choice mattered more than his need.

When they came up for air, they were both panting. "I look forward to learning everything I can about you until the day I die."

He stifled a chuckle as a smirk spread across her face. "Which could have happened tonight and I would have been very upset, so no more listening to Exie's wild ideas." Wrapping her legs around his waist, she ground herself against him, nearly making him lose himself completely. "I didn't wait this long for a mate for him to be taken away before I even got to feel him inside me." Her bluntness set his blood on fire, her need stripping away every wall he might have built.

At that moment, he no longer cared about the War-botach prisoner, or anything beside the female beneath him. In a short amount of time, she'd become the only thing that mattered in his life, and he was okay with that. "Otera can do what she pleases with those prisoners, and I will take your advice on any wild schemes in the future."

"Good," was all she said as she pulled him into another kiss, her hands sliding between them to unbuckle his trousers, the moment a desperate relief when the clasp came loose and her fingers wrapped around his aching cock. "Can you help take these off for me?" She didn't have to ask him twice. His trousers hit the ground next to the bed before she'd even had a chance to move her hand. The cool air barely touched him before her warmth drew him back under.

Chapter Nineteen
Holera

No matter how long they'd known each other, having Kason's skin against hers just felt right, like it was how it should have always been. Every line of his body against hers felt fated, as if the bond had been written into her skin long before they touched. The fact that his body was delicious, well-endowed and with the bulk of a seasoned warrior, only tempted Holera more, making it impossible for her to slow the progression of their night.

Tossing his trousers to the floor, Kason lowered himself over her, his hardened length sliding against her center as he nuzzled into her neck, kissing and licking, the tenderness of the touches setting her aflame. She writhed beneath him, seeking out the friction of his body where she was the most sensitive, the desperate need to be filled consuming her.

Running her fingers up the corded muscles of his back, she luxuriated in the tenderness of his lips on her as he trailed kisses down the column of her neck. His hands explored her curves, cupping her breasts and feeding the taut peak into his mouth. Breath burst out of her when the warmth of his mouth wrapped around her nipple, a surge of pleasure shooting through her body. The sound that tore from her lips was raw, unrestrained, too primal to be contained.

There was no question Kason knew his way around the female form, but she couldn't even spare a moment for jealousy when the culmination of his experience was being used to pleasure her, and would be until he took his last breath. No matter where they'd been before, they'd committed themselves to each other. A mating bond wasn't something their kind took lightly. It was for life. The certainty of that truth wrapped around her as surely as his arms did, steadying her even as her body burned.

"I need you inside of me." Her breath came out as a breathy plea, the rub of his cock against her folds driving her near the edge. "Now."

They had the rest of their lives to take their time, but in that moment, she could no longer wait. Sliding her hand between them, she gripped his cock, fitting it at her entrance. He kissed her as he worked himself inside. The tightness of the fit was exquisite. Her body stretched around him, pleasure and pressure mingling until the line between the two blurred. Relief flooded through her body as Kason's hardness filled her completely. She moaned, every thrust driving her to the edge of ecstasy.

Hooking her leg around his waist, he pulled her against his chest, falling back on his heels as she straddled him. He lifted her, driving his hips up as he pulled her down, the thickness of him forcing the coil low in her belly to twist tighter, threatening to snap.

Slipping her hand in his shoulder-length hair, Holera freed it from the tie binding it and twisted her hand in the thick locks before pulling him to her lips. Kason kissed her deeply, slowing his movements as his tongue caressed hers, the tenderness of it making her moan into his mouth.

Never leaving her body, he laid her back onto her back, his hips rolling into her as her climax built with every thrust. "I want to watch you cum for me," he said as he pulled out of their kiss, the green of his eyes deepening as they locked on hers. "You're so beautiful like this."

His strong hands slid beneath her hips, lifting them slightly, the new angle shattering the coil inside her as her climax hit her with the force of a tidal wave. Her vision blurred, stars sparking behind her eyes as the world narrowed to the heat of his body and the sound of his voice. Sweat dripped from his brow as their eyes remained locked on each other, the intensity of the moment only strengthening her orgasm. The sounds coming from her were loud enough to have been heard from down the hall, but she didn't care.

Burying his face in her neck, Kason's movements became erratic as he reached his own climax, her name on his lips as he collapsed over her. For a few moments, the only sound in the room was heavy breathing as they remained wrapped in each other's arms, trying to catch their breaths. The release drained all of Holera's remaining energy from her and she allowed her eyes to close, falling asleep in her mate's arms for the first time. Safe, claimed, and cherished, she drifted into sleep with his heartbeat steady against her ear.

CHAPTER TWENTY

KASON

Waking up with his mate in his arms and tucked against his chest was how Kason hoped to wake up every morning for the rest of his life. Even with everything that had unfolded at the party, their night together had been perfect. She was everything he could have ever wanted in a female. For the first time in centuries, he felt content, as though fate had finally stopped testing him.

He watched as Holera slept, her chest rising and falling with gentle breaths. Although he knew they needed to get back to the palace, the darkness outside telling him they'd slept through the day, he didn't want to wake her. After only a short time, however, she sighed as she woke, stretching her long limbs and smiling up at him.

Tucking her silver hair behind her ear, Kason leaned forward and kissed her on the cheek. "Good morning, beautiful. How did you sleep?" Holera grinned, pulling him to her and kissing him, her soft lips lingering on his for a long moment, until his cock hardened against her thigh. "After the night we had, I slept like a baby."

At the thought that it was his lovemaking that had made her satisfied enough to sleep well, Kason smirked, the expression purely wicked as he leaned in to kiss her again, this time with unbridled passion.

He groaned against her mouth, the feeling of her tongue against his lips, her tongue, caressing his, only reminding him of how badly he wanted to kiss her in other places. His mate had not been patient the night before and had insisted he sheath himself inside her before he'd been ready. If he'd had it his way, he would have worshiped all of her. He would have kissed every inch of her, worshiped her with his tongue until she cried his name to the rafters, but she had not been patient, therefore he had not been able to taste her yet.

Deciding he couldn't go another moment without having the taste of his mate on his tongue, Kason pulled away from her lips and trailed kisses down her neck, and then moved lower, stopping to kiss and lick her perfect breasts. He settled there for a moment, sliding his body down hers until he could put his face against the pillow softness of her chest and give each of her nipples the attention they deserved. Caressing one with his hand, he fed the other into his mouth and sucked on it gently, twirling his tongue around the tight peak as she moaned and writhed beneath him.

"I was thinking we needed to get back to the palace when we woke," he said, his words no more than a breathy growl. "But then I looked at you and was taken aback by your beauty, and then I remembered that I hadn't gotten to taste you everywhere, so I need to do that before we go anywhere or I may not be able to survive the day."

Holera giggled, bucking her hips as he slid down her body further, settling his shoulders at her thighs. "Are you telling me you would truly die if you didn't taste me this morning, my mate?"

Instead of responding, he decided to show her how badly he wanted to taste her and lifted her leg, putting it over his shoulder and giving himself better access for when he leaned forward, licking her folds, groaning at how perfect the taste of her was. She arched into him, the sound of her pleasure filling the chamber like music meant only for him.

Breath burst out of Holera's beautiful mouth as he licked her a second time, going all the way up to the bundle of nerves and sucking gently on them, knowing that was the spot that would drive her to the edge. "I'm glad to be able to kee-eep you alive then, my ma-te."

Holera's words stuttered out as he devoured her cunt, and the taste of her on his tongue, the smell of her arousal, had him grinding against the bed, desperate to be inside her again. Slipping two fingers into her channel, he licked and sucked on her in steady strokes, knowing exactly what he needed to do to bring her over the edge. "I want you to cum for me, my fierce warrior."

Breathy moans leaving her lips, Holera's hips bucked and writhed as she tried to increase the friction against his face. She fucked his fingers and his tongue until her body stiffened, her legs squeezing around his head as a flood of intoxicating wetness hit his tongue, and she fell limp and panting. The intensity of her release had him gripping her thighs, holding her to his mouth as if he could drink her in forever.

He thought she would need a moment to recover from her orgasm, but as he tried to crawl over her,

Holera pulled him to her, flipping him onto his back and straddling him. Her movements were so desperate, so determined, as she reached between them, gripping his cock in her hand, and sliding down onto it, their bodies fitting together as though they were made for each other. Her silver hair tumbled forward around them like a curtain, her violet eyes blazing with hunger and something deeper—*claiming*.

CHAPTER TWENTY-ONE

HOLERA

Still in an orgasm-induced high, Kason and Holera dressed and made their way back to the palace. Although they would have preferred to remain in bed as a newly-mated couple, they had obligations to their kingdom that couldn't be ignored. The weight of duty pressed heavier than any sleepless night, though Holera couldn't help wishing she was still tangled in Kason's arms. Holera just hoped they were allowed more time alone once the situation with Warbotach was settled.

Arriving back at the palace gates, not only had more guards been posted around the perimeter, but phoenix warriors soared through the sky between the palace and the harbor. The air itself felt tense, thick with the threat of war.

"I was hoping this conflict would be resolved by the time we returned," Holera said, drawing a chuckle out of Kason.

"I was hoping the same, but hopefully a resolution is at least in the works."

Holera nodded as they crossed the lawns of the palace and entered through the front doors as a guard held them open. Although a resolution may have been in the works, which she did not doubt, she also realized any solution would end up being short lived. Warbotach always leaned toward being aggressive in their relations with other kingdoms, and Otera wasn't one to show weakness. Aegricia had to uphold their reputation of being a strong kingdom. Being the only kingdom on their continent ruled by a female, there was always a risk of their land being taken over again.

Traveling down the corridor toward the queen's meeting room, Holera reached for the door handle just as Exie was walking out, nearly knocking her over.

"Oh! Sorry!" Exie said, holding the door open for them to enter. "Where have you two been?"

There had been more than a little mischief in Exie's smirk. Holera scowled at her, not wanting the queen, or anyone else in the room, questioning her personal life. Exie's mischief always came at the worst times, and Holera could feel her cheeks heating under the queen's gaze. Even before she'd had a mate, she'd never been someone who discussed her sex life, aside from with her closest friends.

"I have to deliver a message. I'll be back soon."

Exie darted off before they'd had a chance to respond.

Looking up from the long table that took up much of the room as they entered, the side of Otera's mouth lifted in a strained smile. Her crimson hair caught the lamplight like fire, but the weariness in her eyes betrayed how much the crown cost her. A gentle hand grazed the small of Holera's back as Kason circled behind her and approached the queen's side, peering over the table where a number of parchments and other various items were strewn about.

"Has Warbotach made a move yet?" he asked.

Otera shook her head.
"I just sent a letter to King Uldon, notifying him of the events of the past few days. Their merchant ship has been causing a scene at the harbor, but there has been no more violence."

Loosening a breath, the queen lowered herself onto a chair. "We will let their ship go soon and hope they don't cause any more trouble. The prisoners will be detained for now, although the injured male is in critical condition. He won't be able to travel anytime soon. If it wasn't for their metalworks and glassware, I would cut off trade with Warbotach altogether. Sometimes I wonder if it's worth the stress."

Kason pulled out a chair for Holera to sit just as a servant entered with a decanter, filling their empty glasses. They sat beside each other, leaving little question about their blooming relationship, although Otera paid little mind.

Taking a deep sip of his whiskey, Kason cleared his throat. "If we need to, we could try to establish a trade agreement with one of the other kingdoms to the south, perhaps pay a tax to exchange goods there. I wouldn't recommend going through Diapolis due to the distance and the king's isolationist policies, but Norithae would be willing."

Tapping her fingers on the table, it was clear Otera was debating his suggestion by the way her eyebrows furrowed.

"If we did trade through Norithae, it would benefit Warbotach as well. They wouldn't need to travel as far when making their routes."

Setting her glass back down on the table, Holera watched as Exie walked back into the room and whispered in the queen's ear. Otera listened closely, returning her eyes to Kason as Exie moved aside.

"Blaedia and others are near the harbor. Please inform them to allow the ship to leave—if they're even willing to leave without the others."

Holera's stomach knotted. Letting the Warbotach ship sail away felt too much like loosing a beast back into the wild.

Chapter Twenty-Two

KASON

Sparing not a moment longer, Kason and Holera left the meeting room and headed for the palace court-yard. They made it outside quickly and Holera shifted in a flash of fire, allowing Kason to climb onto her back before launching them into the sky. The wind tore at his hair as they rose, the palace shrinking beneath them, the city bristling with unease. The sun was bright, warming the air and giving Holera's silver wings an ethereal glow.

Soaring through the air, Kason watched as several phoenixes patrolled the city, both on foot and by air. The highest concentration of warriors and guards were in the harbor, at least a dozen surrounding the Warbotach ship as its sailors stormed about the deck, preparing to sail as soon as they were able. The shouts of sailors carried even to their height, sharp and angry, the clatter of crates and chains echoing off the water.

Just as Kason caught sight of Blaedia standing guard near the tree line, Holera leveled her great wings, slowing them as they lowered to the ground.

As soon as Holera's talons met the dirt, Kason slid off her back, waiting at his mate's side as she shifted back into a beautiful, silver-haired female. He watched her as she adjusted her clothes, amazed at how seamlessly she was able to transform from one fierce creature to another. Her silver hair shimmered in the sunlight, every strand gleaming as if dusted with frost. Smoothing out her cloak, she grinned at him, sliding her hand into his as they gave their attention to her general.

Turning toward them, Blaedia sheathed her sword. Another warrior stood by her side. Kason had not yet met the female, but the pin she wore on her cloak's collar told him she was a commander. Her near-silver eyes were sharp and assessing, cool as steel as though she weighed every word before it was spoken.

"Do you bring words from Otera?" Blaedia asked, tension clear on her face. Her jaw was clenched, her hand never straying far from the hilt of her blade. Being the queen's mate could not have been an easy position, especially in times of possible war.

"We just left the palace. The injured prisoner survived surgery, but he is still in critical condition," Holera said, taking her weapons from Kason and securing her bow and quiver over her shoulder, before sheathing her sword. "Otera has sent word to the Warbotach king, letting him know why his two merchants were arrested and detained. The letter also explained that we do not want war. However, we'll be keeping the two prisoners until Otera is satisfied that they were not planning to harm Exie and me when they were caught following us after we'd left the tavern. We have still not been able to discover what their intent was that night. She also said that if the ship is willing to leave without the two prisoners, then they can go back to Warbotach."

"And if they return?" the commander asked, her near-silver eyes scanning them before turning toward the harbor.

"If they return, then we fight."

Pulling her blade back out as though she couldn't decide her next course of action, the general let her arm fall at her side, the tip of her sword digging into the ground.

"Then we should get this over with and go instruct the barbarians of the queen's plans so they can get out of our harbor. I know we would all like to move on with our lives. Kason," she said, turning to look at him. "You'll need to stay behind since you sliced up a few of their men last time you boarded their ship."

Although he hadn't missed the way his mate rolled her eyes, Kason couldn't help but smirk, not because he enjoyed killing, but because the general had said it as though he'd been a naughty child. "It would definitely be best for Exie and I to stay far away from that ship."

When the general turned back to the commander, there was no longer indecision on her face. "You, Holera, and I will go to the ship. With any luck, they'll leave and never come back."

Luck had been in short supply, Holera thought grimly, but she squared her shoulders and followed.

Chapter Twenty-Three
Holera

Kissing Kason goodbye, Holera left her new mate in the forest as she, Taryn, and Blaedia headed toward the harbor on foot. She hadn't wanted to leave him behind, the new bond between them making it nearly impossible for them to be apart. The thread of the mating bond tugged at her chest with every step away from him, a constant reminder of what she was leaving behind. Still, she had a duty to her kingdom as a born warrior, so when Blaedia asked her to provide backup as the Warbotach sailors were notified of the queen's decision, she had no choice but to follow.

Queen Otera's decision was fair, at least from Holera's perspective. Warbotach could leave Aegricia and sail back to their kingdom at the southwestern tip of the continent, but the two prisoners would not be able to join them, not until Otera was satisfied with their explanations of why they'd followed two of her warriors. If the queen believed the merchants had planned to harm her warriors, they would pay with their lives.

Although the harbor had quieted down, the Warbotach merchants now readying their ship instead of antagonizing the Aegrician guards, the area was still filled with a noticeable tension. The air tasted metallic, like the bite of a blade just before it was drawn. It was a difficult situation to manage, and Holera didn't envy her queen in having to navigate it. No matter what decision she made, there would be backlash.

Leading them toward the docks, Blaedia made her way around the guards and warriors stationed there, each with their hands on the hilts of their swords. Their eyes never left the ship, and their bodies were taut as bowstrings.

"I'll go up alone but remain close. I'm hoping the fewer people involved in the resolution, the less likely we'll have pushback."

Taryn and Holera nodded but did not follow their general as she walked up the ramp and toward the deck of the Warbotach ship. If Blaedia felt any unease, it didn't show on her face as she stood only a few feet away from the Warbotach captain.

Noticing the grimace on her commander's face, Holera stifled a grin. Glancing ahead at the barbarian speaking with their general, she knew exactly why Taryn was making such a face, although she hid it well.

Blaedia was so put together, her hair shiny and sharp as a blade, her clothing immaculate. The Warbotach captain, on the other hand, looked as though he'd clawed his way out of a trash heap, hair matted and armor stained with sweat and grime. The barbarian race may have been fae, just like the rest of Ekotoria, but their people couldn't have been more different.

They stood there for several long moments, Holera and Taryn watching over their general as she relayed the queen's message. From the look on the Warbotach male's scarred face, Holera couldn't tell whether he was angry or content. She strained her ears, trying to hear what the two leaders were saying, but their voices did not carry on the breeze. She may have had strong hearing, but they were talking much too low for her to make out any of it.

The longer Blaedia stood in front of the Warbotach ship as the sailors readied the craft to sail in the background, the tighter Holera's chest became. Her hand drifted to the hilt of her sword, though she knew steel would be too slow if the captain chose violence. They may have been surrounded by armed guards, but it would only take a second for the Warbotach captain to strike against their general, and they were too far away to stop it.

In the corner of her eye, Holera watched as Taryn shifted on her feet, the commander clearly growing restless as well. When she turned her eyes back to the ship, Holera's blood turned to ice as her fear was realized. Blaedia no longer stood face-to-face with the ship's captain. Instead, he had her back flush against his chest, a blade held to her throat. Holera's stomach dropped. Every muscle in her body screamed to act, but the distance between them might as well have been a canyon. The barbarians were going to try to hold her hostage.

CHAPTER TWENTY-FOUR

KASON

Kason clenched his teeth as his mate walked away and into the danger brewing in the harbor. Although he'd wanted to follow her, he knew it would have only put her at more risk. Every instinct in his body screamed to follow her, but instinct had to bow to reason. After he and Exie had created chaos on the Warbotach ship, killing two of their people and capturing another, he knew his presence would only anger them more.

Straining his eyes to see into the distance, he watched the entire scene unfold. He saw how the Warbotach captain had flipped Blaedia's back against him and pressed a dagger against her throat. With the general's extensive fighting and negotiation skills, he trusted Blaedia enough to know surrender was part of her strategy, not weakness. He didn't know what had been discussed in their conversation, but he believed she had a plan.

Hands clenched into fists at his side, Kason fought the urge to sprint toward the harbor and protect his mate, but before he'd had the chance to take that first step, Holera turned, her long legs sprinting forward and racing back in his direction. Her braid streamed behind her like a silver banner, her face carved with resolve.

"What the fuck happened?" The words left his lips as soon as his mate's eyes met his, the violet blazing to a near silver in the sun. There was so much tension in her face that he regretted his demanding words.

"There's no time for explanations," she responded, checking that her weapons were secure at her back before placing a kiss on his lips. "Taryn wants us to follow the ship. Shoot to kill, but don't endanger Blaedia."

Although Kason knew the general would have never wanted them to endanger more warriors at her expense, he nodded.

Without another word, his mate shifted into her phoenix form, dipping her head low for him to climb onto her back. Only a moment later, she launched them into the air.

Notching an arrow in his bow, Kason spotted the Warbotach ship in the distance, the wind and current having already taken it miles offshore. Other phoenixes already soared in the sky around the craft, but Blaedia was no longer visible.

"They must have taken her below deck," he said. Holera couldn't respond in her phoenix form, but she could hear him.

Her wings flared, taking them higher into the clouds. Circling the ship from a safe distance, away from the arrows sailing into the sky from below, Kason scanned the upper decks, looking for the general and counting the ship's crew.

No less than thirty armed sailors moved around the craft. The deck bristled with blades and bows, a wall of bodies ready to kill rather than yield. All thoughts of peace were over as they launched their arrows at the Aegricians. The phoenix warriors were well-trained, agile as they dove and circled, the arrows missing their targets every time. Each beast held a rider, someone on their back, using their weapons to dispatch the enemy below.

An arrow narrowly missed Holera's wing and Kason screamed, alerting her just in time to fly out of the way. The shaft grazed so close he swore he felt the wind of it across his cheek. His arrow shot toward the male who had tried to harm his mate, hitting him in the eye before he'd even had a chance to know he had become a target.

Caressing the feathers on Holera's neck, Kason leaned forward to kiss her. "There's no one on the eastern side of the deck. Swoop low and I'll jump onto the ship to look for Blaedia."

Fierce eyes met his as his mate's beautiful phoenix head looked back at him, a look telling him he was crazy and she didn't approve. The bond between them thrummed with her resistance, a silent roar of her disapproval.

Kason chuckled, amusement filling his eyes at the stubbornness of his new mate. "I'll be fine. In and out. You can swoop down and pick me up in a few minutes and then we can go back to my room so I can worship you."

CHAPTER TWENTY-FIVE

HOLERA

Although Holera hated the idea of her mate going back on the Warbotach ship, she had to admit that finding a way on the craft was the best way to get Blaedia back. With all the phoenixes circling over the ship, the Warbotach merchants had their eyes on the sky, shooting arrows at the massive birds. There were very few of the enemy paying attention to the deck itself, especially the rear. Still, Holera's chest tightened. Every instinct screamed to shield her mate, not deliver him back into the viper's den.

Letting out a call the other phoenix warriors would understand, Holera flared her wings, taking them into the sky and away from the chaotic scene. Before she could land on the back of the ship, she had to make sure all eyes were off her. Lowering them into the trees, she did just that.

Holera landed on the ground, needing to shift back into her fae form quickly so she and Kason could talk about their plan. As soon as she landed on the leaf-littered ground, the scent of damp earth and pine clung to the clearing, grounding her for a heartbeat before the storm ahead. Her mate jumped off her back. She shifted a moment later.

Slinging his bow over his back, Kason grinned at her as he closed the distance between them and pulled her into a kiss. She submitted fully to him, knowing it could be the last time he held her if their rescue attempt went wrong. The thought sliced through her resolve, making her cling harder, memorizing the heat of his mouth.

When they parted, Holera was breathless.
"We need to come up with a plan. I don't like the idea of sending you onto that ship again, not after what happened last time."

Kason grinned, the gesture filled with confidence.
"I'll be fine. I have too much to live for now." The conviction in his tone steadied her even as it infuriated her, because she knew he meant her.

Wrapping his muscular arm around her waist, he pulled her in close again, kissing her on the neck. The intimate touch made her want to pull down his pants and ride him right where they stood, but her obligation to Blaedia urged her to pull away.

"We'll try to sneak up on the ship, but I'm going with you."

Before she'd even finished her statement, Kason was already shaking his head.
"Let me go in alone while you circle to the south. I won't be long. There's no reason to put you in danger, my fierce warrior."

Just the thought of sending him in alone turned her stomach.
"I'll stay on the back deck and keep watch, but I'm not leaving that ship without you." Her voice was iron. No amount of persuasion would move her from his side.

Before he could argue, Holera shifted back into her phoenix form, nuzzling her beak into his leg. He stroked her feathers, smirking as he climbed onto her back.
"Although I've only known you for a short time, I feel like I'll never win an argument with you."

She couldn't laugh in her phoenix form, but she let out a chitter as she spread her great silver wings and launched them into the air.

Soaring above the tree canopy, Holera cut further to the south, her silver wings nearly invisible in the gray sky as she aimed like a dart for the back of the ship. As had been the case before, all the Warbotach sailors were near the front of the ship. The phoenixes continued to fly in an unpredictable pattern while their riders fired arrows at the enemy. She watched as one of her friends, Andrianna, dove toward the bow of the ship, plucking up one of the Warbotach males and dropping him into the sea.

Swooping low over the water, Holera lifted them just as they neared the rear of the ship, landing on the deck with a near silent thump. Kason slid off her back, drawing his sword from its sheath and scanning their surroundings. The planks groaned beneath their boots, the smell of salt and tar thick in the air. Every shadow felt like an enemy waiting to strike. Holera shifted, standing on the tips of her toes and kissing her mate on the lips.

"If you make it back to me safely, I'll suck your cock when we get back to the room."

Giving her one more heated look, a growl rumbled out of Kason's chest as he crept toward the stairs that would lead him to the lower deck.

CHAPTER TWENTY-SIX

KASON

Leaving his mate on the back deck and hoping no Warbotach scum found her there, Kason moved on silent feet toward the stairs that would lead him below deck. The bond thrummed faintly at his chest, Holera's presence tugging like a lifeline even as he forced himself away from her. With the total chaos on the front of the ship, no one seemed to notice him as he disappeared into the darkened stairwell. Well, he hoped no one noticed.

Although Kason had been on a merchant ship before, the shadowed space was difficult to map out. Peeking inside each door on the first level as he passed, Kason quickly realized that Blaedia was probably locked up on a lower level. He also realized the more levels below deck he went, the more likely he would get caught.

Scanning the corridor around him and not seeing anyone, Kason turned the doorknob for the stairs that would lead him to the lower levels. The door let out a low squeal as he shut it behind himself and headed down the narrow staircase.

With as broad as his shoulders were, claustrophobia hit him quickly, tightening his breaths, but he continued to descend. They always made his lungs fail to pull in enough oxygen. Sweat broke across his brow, not from heat but from the walls pressing too close.

The smell of musk and urine hit him hard as he rounded the last turn into the bowels of the ship. The reek clawed down his throat, making his stomach lurch as bile threatened to rise. Fighting the urge, Kason took the candle closest to the stairs and stepped further into the dank, dark space. With no light from windows, the lowest level of the craft was heavily shadowed, making it difficult to see. He passed each crate and barrel, remaining vigilant just in case an enemy was waiting to ambush him.

As he approached the back of the space, the hold appeared, the figure of a female standing inside.

"Blaedia?" Keeping his voice at a whisper, he took the last remaining steps forward toward the cage the Aegrician general was being held in. "Are you okay?"

She jolted at the sound of his voice, her silver eyes wide as she met his. Aside from blood dripping from a gash on her arm and a busted lip, Blaedia appeared to be unharmed. Her stance was still proud, her gaze unbroken—the look of a warrior who would die on her feet before she begged. With her fae blood, the wounds she had would heal quickly.

"Kason? What are you doing here?" Although he would have expected the general to be relieved to see him, she seemed agitated. "Please don't tell me my military is putting lives at risk for me. They know better." Her tone cracked like a whip, even weakened, as though discipline itself kept her upright.

Kason chuckled as he fumbled with the lock on her cell. "They may know better, but even if they refused to go after you, the queen wouldn't have let Warbotach take you."

Just thinking about Holera being in that cage, Kason knew he would've made the same decision. The thought made his blood boil; he would have burned the ship to ash to keep her safe.

The cell was locked, but he had become a master at picking locks, so it only took him a minute and a small tool from his pocket before the door swung open. Not hesitating for a moment, Blaedia stepped out of the cage.

"They've got my weapons," she said, reaching for a sword that wasn't there.

Pulling a short sword from the scabbard at his waist, Kason handed it to her. "I can't guarantee we'll find yours, but you can use this one for now."

Blaedia took the weapon, holding it at the ready as they began walking toward the stairway, but before they took more than a few steps, muffled voices met Kason's ears.

Grabbing Blaedia by the arm, he pulled her behind a stack of crates, quieting his breaths as they watched the bottom of the stairway, waiting to see who came inside. Every second stretched, the shadows heavy with the promise of violence.

CHAPTER TWENTY-SEVEN
HOLERA

While Kason crept below deck, Holera remained on the back of the ship, crouching behind crates to observe the chaos on the bow. She believed that all Warbotach merchants were entangled with the phoenixes pursuing them from the air. When an arm grabbed her from behind, and a dagger's blade pressed into her neck, she was completely caught off guard. Her heart slammed in her chest, her body jerking with the shock of cold steel at her throat.

"Well, well. Aren't you a pretty thing?" he snarled, forcing her to step forward. "Walk, cunt. Let's go get reunited with your general."

Despite her desire to fight back, Holera knew better. In such a vulnerable position, she would die if she lashed out. She had too much to live for to be reckless. The bond to her mate thrummed in her chest, a tether she refused to let be cut.

With the Warbotach beast's blade at her throat, she took small steps toward the stairway leading to the lower decks. As she took each step down, she held her back straight to prevent her flesh from being cut by his knife.

Throughout the lower decks, they passed several doors, but the man behind Holera kept leading her forward into the ship's deepest interior.

In the dark, her attention was fixed on the level below them as they neared the opening to the bottom. Assuming the dungeons were on this level, she hoped Kason had managed to free their general by the time she and her captor entered. As she took those last few steps and the floor of the dungeon came into view, her ears almost missed the hushed conversation of her general and her mate.

When Holera realized Kason and Blaedia were still there, her heart flipped. They had not escaped. In a last desperate effort to stall, Holera shoved her butt back into the male behind her, nearly sending him to the ground. Blood trickled down her throat where the blade had dug in just enough to cut her.

"Stand up straight and walk, you dumb cunt," he growled, the beast's hot breath smelling of stale whiskey as it flickered across her cheek, nearly making her vomit.

After walking into the dungeon with the male behind her, Holera peered into the darkness. When she looked for her mate and her general, they weren't there, or at least they weren't visible. Her relief lasted only for a moment as the male behind her leapt forward, cursing and pushing her to the ground. As the guard approached the cage where Blaedia had been kept, now empty, he growled and swung his fist at the metal, and it shuddered. A reverberating sound filled the cavernous space. The metallic clang rolled through the shadows, echoing like a death knell.

He turned his eyes to Holera and moved toward her like he wanted to kill her. Pulling her dagger from its sheath at her thigh, she skittered back, trying to get back to her feet. Before he reached her, an arrow flew through the air from the other side of the room and struck the beast in the temple. The arrow pierced his temple with a sickening crack, snapping his snarl into silence as his body collapsed in a boneless heap, his eyes staring at her vacantly. Her enemy lying motionless at her feet, she breathed a sigh of relief.

As soon as her attacker fell, Kason's broad shoulders moved out from behind a stack of crates. He closed the space between them in an instant and pulled her into his arms.

"We have to get out of here," he said. "Fast. Blaedia has a plan, but we need to get off the ship as soon as possible."

Holera's heart beat like a war drum. On the ground behind Kason, Blaedia lined up bottles that she had pulled out of a crate.

As she moved forward to assist her general with whatever task she was trying to accomplish, she asked, "What's the plan?" All three of them needed to get off the ship as soon as possible, and she didn't understand why they were stalling, but if Blaedia had a plan, she wanted to help.

Blaedia's silver eyes were filled with pure determination as she looked at her. "You and Kason need to get off the ship. That's an order," Blaedia said in a tone that accepted no arguments. She looked at her warrior again a moment later, her eyes softening. "No need to worry, Holera. Yes, I'll get off too, but not before I light the ship on fire. There is no way these bastards are leaving Aegricia. When I leave this ship, they will burn and sink into the sea." Her voice was calm, but the steel in her silver eyes promised she would see it done, even if it meant burning with it.

Without further explanation, Kason grabbed Holera's hand and guided her to the stairs. Within a few seconds, they were back on the top deck.

Holera morphed into a phoenix and launched into the air with her mate on her back. As she flew, her massive silver wings worked hard to deliver her around the arrows flying overhead and to the rest of the phoenixes.

She gave a loud cry, ordering the rest of the phoenixes to abandon the attack. As Holera moved out of the reach of the arrows, they followed without argument.

By the time Holera and Kason reached a safe distance and turned around to make sure their general had gotten off the ship safely, the giant black and crimson phoenix was already flying toward them, leaving the ship ablaze behind her. For a heartbeat, Holera's breath caught — their general was more than a warrior; she was retribution made flesh and flame. In the blink of an eye, Blaedia had already caught up with them, her wingspan creating a majestic silhouette against the bright orange flames of the burning ship.

CHAPTER TWENTY-EIGHT

KASON

Once there was nothing left of the Warbotach ship but smoke trails in the air, nearly everyone had been swept up in damage control. After an extensive meeting with her top officials, Queen Otera agreed with the idea of fabricating an alternative story. She wanted to keep the truth from the enemy, so she announced that the ship had been lost at sea. Trusting their queen, the citizens accepted her story, though some may have been skeptical. The truth of what had happened remained a secret between the Queen and her advisors. Secrets this heavy had a way of surfacing eventually, but for now the lie gave Aegricia the illusion of safety.

The plan could only work if they were able to prevent her earlier message from reaching the Warbotach king, so Blaedia sent the fastest phoenix to intercept it, while the rest of their plan was put into place. Since the harbor had been blocked off by a perimeter of Aegrician guards and warriors, most of the people in the capital city, locals and travelers alike, had not seen what had happened over the water. With that hope in mind, an Aegrician ship was sent south with meticulous instructions on how to lay a false trail, to make it look as though the Warbotach craft had sunk on the high seas. With any luck, it would work. Still, Kason couldn't shake the feeling of unease whenever he looked east, toward the sea, as if the waves themselves carried whispers of vengeance.

He hoped Otera's plan would hold, but he knew better than to trust fragile peace. Conflict was always a tide—it came back eventually. When it did, Aegricia would need to be ready. For now, though, he and Holera needed time to themselves.

On the fourth day after the sinking of the enemy ship, Kason and Holera left Flamecliff behind, intending to take some time away. They headed to Holera's family home so he could meet her mother. Becoming mated was one of the most pivotal moments in a fae's life, and forging ties with her family was important. The thought made him more anxious than any battle—winning a mother's approval was a war of its own.

As they arrived in front of the wooden cottage, the sky was colored in an array of pastel shades accented by fluffy white clouds. The snow on the mountains had started to melt, but there were still white caps on the tallest peaks. A small stream cascaded down the side of the mountain, the sound of its running waters reminding him of a lullaby. For the first time in a long time, there was peace in the air.

Holera shifted back into her fae form, and Kason immediately moved to her side, taking her weapons and holding them for her as she led the way to the front door. The door swung open before they could touch the knob, and a tall silver-haired female stood in the doorway. Her violet eyes glistened with tears, and even before she spoke, Kason knew this was Holera's mother.

"Oh! I was so worried!" she cried as she closed the distance and pulled Holera into her arms. Watching them, Kason felt something stir in his chest. His mate was his everything, and seeing her loved so fiercely by her mother filled him with warmth. It also carved an ache in him, a reminder that he had no family left.

They stayed like that for a few moments until the matriarch finally let go. Wiping her eyes, she turned her attention to him. A grin spread across her face, and as if to say she approved, she gave him a knowing nod. Kason straightened unconsciously, pride stirring in his chest.

"I thought I'd smelled a mate bond on my daughter," she said as she squeezed Holera's hands and smiled at them both, unconditional love in her eyes. "Should congratulations be in order, my beloved daughter? Who is this handsome male you've brought home to meet me?"

Holera stepped aside, raising one of her hands to take his. "Kason, this is my mother, Aura. Mother, I would like you to meet Kason, my mate."

Beaming with a brilliant smile, Aura stepped forward. Her irises were a darker violet than Holera's but no less enchanting. She reached out and wrapped her arms around Kason. He stiffened for the briefest moment, unaccustomed to such maternal warmth, then let himself sink into it. For a male who had spent decades with no family, her embrace nearly undid him. When Aura stepped back, her eyes were bright with joy.

"I am so glad to meet you, Kason. I've been hoping for Holera to find a suitable male for a long time. If the bond has clicked into place, then you surely must be the finest of males."

Her words, spoken without hesitation, sank deep into him—a blessing more powerful than any oath.

EPILOGUE

KASON

Having spent two days with Holera's mother, Kason and Holera set off for his cabin in the mountains for the first time. In the short time since they'd met, he'd told her about his cabin, but was looking forward to showing it to her. In addition, he was looking forward to spending some time alone with her. The excitement in his heart was palpable as they crested the last cliff, soaring through the clouds on her magnificent silver wings, and he captured the first glimpse of his property.

"We're home, my fierce warrior," he said as he stroked the feathers on her neck, then leaned forward to kiss her. Making the cooing sound that was her approval, she bent her head back to rub it on his knee.

Minutes later, they landed near the creek on the edge of his land, and he dismounted, standing aside as she transformed into her stunning fae form. Closing the distance between them, he lifted her into his arms and pressed his lips to hers. A spark of electricity coursed through his veins the moment she melted against him. A fire ignited in his heart every time she touched him; one he knew would never go out. He pulled away reluctantly, her kiss leaving him breathless as he hurried to the front door.

Holera giggled, stroking his hair that had broken loose from its tie. "Are you excited about something, my mate?"

With a grunt, he turned the knob and stormed inside, kicking the door shut behind him. "You told me you would suck my cock once the battle was over." His words were shameless, but he didn't care. Although she laughed harder, he was not deterred. Passing through the rooms, he did not stop to give her a tour before entering his bed chamber.

"So that's what all the rush is about? You think I'm going to suck your cock? Well..." She paused just long enough to make his stomach clench. "That's what I said, isn't it?"

Upon entering the room, he kicked off his boots and set her down on the bed. She pulled her tunic over her head and tossed it to the ground, her face pure feline mischief. "What would you be willing to do for me?"

Chuckling, he tossed his weapons on the floor, not paying attention to where they landed before dropping his tunic beside them. "My beautiful mate, I will do anything and everything to make you happy."

To his surprise, she scooted forward on the bed, unclasping his trousers' buckle before pulling them down his hips. Already pulsing with need, his cock sprung free. A flare of excitement filled her eyes as she dipped her head closer and rubbed her tongue over the length of his shaft.

"Is this what you want?" she purred as she leaned forward and wrapped her mouth around its swollen tip, the feeling of it forcing a gasp from deep in his chest.

Unable to form words, he nodded and slipped his fingers into her hair, pulling the band out so that her silver locks flowed freely across her back.

His hands fisted in her hair as her lips encased him, squeezing and licking and drawing out a guttural moan of pleasure. His hips bucked, pushing against her eager mouth as his balls tightened, his body racing toward climax.

Although he'd always prided himself on having good stamina, he knew if she didn't stop immediately, he was going to spill his seed into her mouth. He tried to pull away so he could get his head between her legs and devour her until she climaxed first, but she wouldn't let him.

With her arms around him, she clung to his backside and pulled him closer, sucking and caressing him with her exquisite mouth until he was on the verge of exploding. He clenched his teeth, trying to delay the inevitable, but he couldn't.

"Stop. I'm about to," he huffed out, but she shook her head, eyes flicking up to look at him as her lips stretched around his member. She wanted to taste him, and he didn't think he could have loved her more.

As she massaged his balls, she sucked him in deeper, his cock hitting the back of her throat. It was too much for him to bear. His orgasm hit him like lightning, breaking apart on the inside of his body, sending his eyes rolling back in his head as he rode the waves of it. As he emptied himself into her mouth, she licked up every drop, seeming to savor the taste of him as he did with her. Completely spent and panting, he collapsed back onto the bed and she crawled up beside him, a satisfied smirk on her face. He kissed her passionately, their tongues intertwining as he pulled her closer, still trembling from his pleasure but ready for more.

Although they would face hardships in their lives and in their kingdom, in that moment, he intended to deliver the most intense orgasm she had ever experienced. After that, the future was still uncertain, but he knew that whatever lay ahead, they would get through it together.

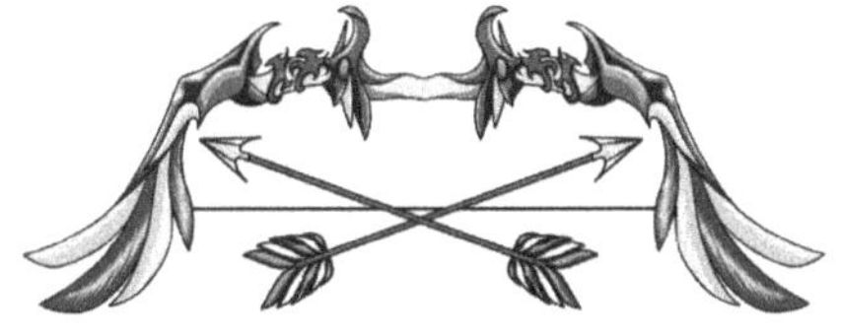

"Are you sure we need all this stuff?" Kason asked as he shoveled another load of dirt into the rows Holera had dug for her new garden project. "You know I can hunt, right?"

His fiery mate looked at him like he'd said the most idiotic thing she'd heard all day. "I'm aware you can hunt, my oh-so helpful and very sexy mate, but I eat more than just meat. If you want me to live here part of the year, I need something other than things that bleed for nourishment."

Chuckling, he pulled the already sweaty rag from his pocket and wiped his forehead as he watched her bend over the dirt to smooth it out.

"You know, if you want to take a break…" Moving in close behind her, he tried to slide his arms around her waist to spin her around, but she tossed a handful of dirt back at him, hitting him in the face. Her shoulders shook as she stifled her laughter, but the dirt to the face hadn't been a deterrent.

Wiping his face again, he wrapped his arms around her and pulled her to the ground.

"Kason! No! I'm trying to finish this before dinner."

Ignoring her protests, he slid his dirty fingers into her hair and pulled her lips to his. "You'll have the rest of our lives to make our home perfect, and I'll always help to ease your burden."

ENJOYING HOLERA AND KASON'S STORY?

If you enjoyed this book, please leave a review!

Reviews are vital to authors! They help books reach new readers. I really appreciate it!

Leave a review here:
https://www.amazon.com/Mate-Phoenix-Crown-Prequel-Novella-ebook/dp/B0BYY21GB9

Sign up for C. A. Varian's newsletter to receive current updates on her new and upcoming releases, sales, and giveaways:
https://sendfox.com/cavarian

You can also find all my books and social media pages here:
https://cavarian.com/

CROWN OF THE PHOENIX

C.A. VARIAN

CHAPTER I

VAEKROS

"Aurelia, you'll never defend yourself swinging like that. Are you even trying?"

Aurelia wiped the sweat from her brow and tightened her grip on her sword, swinging at Amadeus's larger blade, only for him to slap hers to the ground. She grunted.

"It's not a fair fight, you know. Your blade is bigger, and I am a girl!"

Her brother snorted, bracing his feet in a defensive stance.

"Blade size shouldn't matter. If anything, a smaller blade should be lighter—easier to maneuver."

"Room for me?" Septima called as she strolled across the training grounds. Just as Amadeus turned to look at their sister, Aurelia slammed her sword into his, forcing it from his hands. It clattered loudly as it hit the grass.

"Hey!" His outraged shriek held little threat with Aurelia's blade now leveled with his gut. "I wasn't ready."

Waiting until she thought he just may urinate on himself, she smirked and lowered her weapon to her side. "Horse's backside, Amadeus."

Dropping her sword, Aurelia ran to Septima, wrapping her arm around her sister's shoulder. "We have room for you, but I doubt you want to fight against that old nag's tail." She flipped her thumb over her shoulder, pointing at their brother, who rolled his eyes.

"I'll fight you then," Septima said as she darted for Amadeus' sword, swiping it from the ground, and wielding it in her sister's direction.

Aurelia retrieved her blade and swung it at Septima, only for her strike to be blocked. Her jaw dropped as Septima sneered at her. When her look morphed into a mischievous one, Aurelia braced herself for retaliation.

Amadeus began walking toward the house. "I'm going to head home. I'll grab my sword later. Have fun and try not to cut off each other's ears."

The sisters barely paid attention to him as their eyes remained on one another, waiting for the next move to be taken. Septima circled left, waving her weapon in arcs. Taking a step back, Aurelia dropped her weapon on the ground and took off running toward the gardens. She was tired of sparring, and leading a chase was far more fun. Glancing over her shoulder, she noticed Septima in pursuit, her lips spread into a bright smile.

Once they entered the gardens, the pair fell to the ground and began giggling uncontrollably. They lay among the flowers, admiring the cloudless sky and the breeze rolling off the Harmuz Sea. The sea, ever crashing against the weather-beaten white cliffs, carved dramatic rock faces. Though the cliffs were too high to climb down for a swim, the view was magnificent. Lying in the gardens, overlooking the water below, was one of their favorite pastimes.

"It must be such a thrill," Septima said, rolling onto her side to face Aurelia. Her dark eyes shone in the sunlight and her long ebony braids shimmered like black silk.

Aurelia turned to face her sister, twirling a yellow wildflower between her fingers. "What would be a thrill?"

The longing for adventure played across Septima's features. "To fight... to be a fearless warrior. I'm sick of being expected to be a proper lady who spends her time doing tedious things."

Sighing, Aurelia flicked the flower toward her sister. It landed near her hand. "Father would never allow it. You know we are to be wed. It's what is expected of us. I'm surprised he hasn't married me off yet. My twenty-first birthday will be here soon." The number felt heavy on her tongue. Twenty-one, and still waiting for her father to decide her fate. She knew why her sister wanted to seek adventure instead of marriage, but she did not know how to help make that happen for her. It was something she thought about often, knowing Septima did not fancy men at all. She was only attracted to women, but marrying the same sex was not allowed in Vaekros. Neither were women warriors. The options to bring her sister happiness were slim, and that was heartbreaking.

Rolling her eyes, Septima turned onto her back to gaze at the sky. "I'm not getting married to a man, expectations or not."

Aurelia's chest tightened at her sister's plight. "Marrying a woman isn't an option in Vaekros. You know that."

Septima's voice sharpened to steel. "That may be true, but I will not be forced to marry a man. I'd sooner die, Lia. I swear it."

Aurelia's chest ached at her sister's words, not just for the danger of defying their father, but for the quiet truth between them: she wanted to love freely, and their world had no place for that. Aurelia wanted to promise she'd find a way. Still, she had no answers, only the ache of knowing Septima's cage was tighter than her own.

Instead of responding, Aurelia bit her lip and turned to stare at the sky as well. They lay in silence for a while, neither knowing how to continue the conversation. They did not know how to solve a problem that had no solution in their society.

After a moment, Aurelia stood and dusted off her clothes. "I'm going to go check on Kano. He needs to get out of the house before he shreds up everything in it. I'll catch up with you a bit later." She leaned over to give her sister a kiss on the cheek before heading toward the house. Septima waved as she walked away.

Reluctantly rising from the flowers, Aurelia brushed the dirt from her clothes. The carefree afternoon had ended; the villa loomed ahead, full of its shadows and rules.

While Septima was not Aurelia's sister by blood, she was the single most important person in her life. Aurelia's father had found Septima when she was only a baby, while his army lay siege to El-Wahba. Septima's father had been killed in the attack, and her mother had been enslaved. Aurelia's parents became Septima's, although they could not have been more different in appearance.

While on campaign to foreign lands, Septima was not the only baby their father saved and brought back to their home in Vaekros. He had also given Aurelia a tiger cub. Her beautiful Kano, who, aside from Septima, was her best friend. She remembered it like it was yesterday. She was less than two years old when she met her baby sister, but was ten years old when the tiny cub was placed in her arms. She named him for the Sun God, for his striped fur shimmered gold like sunlight on water. He'd been a runt, a fragile cub no one believed would live, but under her care, he had grown into strength. To others, he was a beast to be shunned; to Aurelia, he was everything—guardian, confidant, and the only warmth in a house that too often felt like a prison.

As Aurelia moved across the grounds, she approached the villa through the back door. She adored the home, which was dramatically situated along the rocky cliffs near the Howling Mountains and Forest. The seaside estate, adorned with mosaics and frescoes, was designed around a sunlit atrium. Servants lived in a separate stone building at the edge of the property. A small wooden cottage, also located on the outskirts of the estate, belonged to Amadeus, who was still unmarried.

The stone atrium was filled with a variety of potted trees, vines, and flowers. A large pool sparkled in its center—a pool the girls frequented in the warmer months since reaching the sea was impossible from the height of the house.

Inside, polished marble gleamed across endless rooms—reception halls, bathing chambers, even a grand library, each space immaculate under Proteus's exacting rule. To others, it might seem like a palace. To Aurelia, it often felt like a barracks, patrolled by a commander instead of a father. Discipline lived in every stone of the house, but warmth had long since died with her mother.

When Aurelia entered her bedchamber, Kano stretched his massive body and slinked up to her to nuzzle her legs. She dropped into the vanity seat and untangled her braid while she gazed at herself in the bronze mirror. Her large blue eyes and crimson hair were such a contrast to Septima's long midnight braids and her deep tawny skin.

Some said her red hair was a gift from Veena, the Goddess of Life and Death. Not unlike the goddess, Aurelia loved to spar. She loved learning to wield weapons, even if it was all but forbidden in her society. She had to be a respectable Vaekrosan lady, and that meant never making a man feel weak in her presence. Even so, she sparred with her brother and with Septima to practice her swordsmanship. With as many fights as Vaekros picked, she never knew when such skills would be helpful.

Aurelia turned to admire her bedchamber. The aqua walls mirrored the sea, catching sunlight in the tall windows so the room glowed like water. A huge four-poster bed took up a large part of the suite, large enough for Kano to sleep alongside her and keep her warm.

Beyond her window rose her favorite sight, the Marella Arch, carved by the sea into a jagged portal of stone. Some in Vaekros called it cursed, others blessed, but Aurelia clung to the version from her dreams: a doorway to freedom, a world beyond her father's reach. Yet whenever the waves struck its base, foaming like teeth in a dark maw, she wondered if it promised escape... or demanded sacrifice.

Curled up like a mountain at her feet, Kano let out a mighty snore. She reached over and caressed his sleek fur, rousing him from his slumber. He yawned wide, fangs flashing in the light, his amber eyes heavy with sleepy yet watchful, as if he alone sensed what the house concealed. Rising to his feet, he rubbed against the cloth of her pants as she rubbed his head.

"You're being lazy today, Kano. I think it's time for us to play outside."

He bobbed his head like he understood her. Leaving her chambers with the great cat trailing behind her, Aurelia took the stairs quickly to look for Septima and sunshine.

After searching the villa twice over, she found both at the same time. Septima sat on a stone bench in the rose garden, soaking in the sun and reading a book. Kano sprinted at the sight of her, nuzzling his enormous head against Septima's legs. She giggled, ruffling his fur.

"Hey there, big guy," she said, placing a kiss on his head before gleaming a toothy grin at Aurelia. "What are you two up to?"

Aurelia shrugged, dropping to sit beside her. "Kano has been too lazy today. I thought a game of hide and seek would be good for him. Do you want to play?"

Septima chuckled. "Aren't we a little old for such games?"

Rising from the bench, Aurelia straightened her tunic. "I'm older, and I still play." She shrugged. "Let's go, Kano, the last one in the forest is a horse's backside."

Running as fast as she could, Aurelia darted into the tree line. The sound of Kano's enormous paws thudded close behind her.

The forest was vast, dense, and rich. Its canopy comprised pine, Buxus, and holly. Enough light shimmered through their crowns for a medley of shrubs to take advantage of the fertile grounds below. Silent vines suspended from many trees, and a range of flowers, which grew in a sprinkled, disorderly fashion, brightened up the otherwise homogeneous scenery. A mishmash of noises, predominantly those of critters, echoed throughout and were backed by the occasional sounds of birds of prey gliding in the air.

Aurelia laughed as she ran, climbing into an abandoned hollow just big enough for her to fit. Holding her breath, she knew he could smell her, but he seemed to pretend he couldn't, like he knew the rules of the game.

Quick footsteps paced in the distance. She pulled herself as far into the tree as she could, hoping there weren't any rodents nesting in there that would bite her like last time.

"Got you!" Septima's braids fell into the hollow, nearly slapping her in the face. They both began giggling as Kano bounded up to them as they kneeled, licking their faces.

Aurelia wiped the slobber off her cheek with the back of her hand. "I thought you were too old for this game?"

Septima shrugged as she wiped her own face. "You know I'll be playing in the forest with you even when my hair turns gray, especially with this big guy." She reached out and scratched Kano behind his ear. He leaned into her.

They played for hours. Each taking great care in where they hid, only for Kano to find them each time.

Dirt clung to their clothes as the sisters and Kano trudged back toward the villa, the sinking sun setting the Howling Mountains aflame. Before the threshold emerged from the shadows, Kano stiffened, ears pressed flat, a rumble rising from his chest. Aurelia's hand skimmed his fur in a futile attempt to calm him, even as unease coiled in her stomach. Then she looked up. Her father waited in the foyer with two strangers at his side, and her heart dropped like a stone.

CHAPTER 2

AEGRICIA

Otera dragged her feet as the cloaked brute hauled her through the depths of the dungeon, iron fingers digging into her arm. The air was bone-chilling, her thin nightdress clinging uselessly to her damp skin. Every step scraped her bare feet against the rough stone.

"You don't have to drag me," she snapped, though the tremor in her voice betrayed her. "I can walk on my own."

He grunted in response and yanked harder, bruising her flesh.

The dungeons beneath her castle had rarely been used. Only the most dangerous criminals ever rotted here, and even they did not linger long. The cells were damp, foul, and unfit for beasts, let alone a queen. Never had Otera imagined she would be the one cast behind these bars.

The Warbotach cavalry had come swiftly, their siege forcing her hand: open the gates or see innocents slaughtered. Her military had not abandoned her; they had retreated to build strength, gather allies, and return when the time was right. That had been the plan when word of Norithae's invasion first reached them weeks ago. But knowing the plan did little to soothe the gnawing weight of uncertainty.

And so, she endured, captive in her own fortress. Uldon, the Warbotach leader, wanted her crown and power, but he could not spill her blood to gain them. Her life was guaranteed; her dignity, however, was not.

Shoved into the stone-walled dark, Otera stumbled to the straw pallet in the corner as the iron door clanged shut. The echo rattled down the corridor until only silence remained.

She pressed her hands against the damp wall, as if she might still feel the heartbeat of her kingdom through its bones. But there was nothing, only the stench of mildew and the faint drip of water echoing like a slow clock.

Uldon fancied himself clever, demanding her crown without spilling her blood. He thought stripping her of comfort would make her weak. Yet Otera knew that crowns could be stolen, but loyalty could not. Her people's faith in her would outlast his tyranny.

The silence pressed harder than any shout, filling the void with memories of voices she would give anything to hear again—the laughter of her warriors, the songs sung in Flamecliff's halls. Now there was only stone, straw, and the slow rot of time.

She hated that the Warbotach could cage her body, but they could not cage her will. Her crown was not made of iron or gold; it was the fire that still burned inside her.

And so, she sat in the gloom with nothing but a slit of light high in the wall and her thoughts, sharp as chains.

CHAPTER 3

VAEKROS

Proteus's eyes swept over the dirt on his daughters' clothes, his lip curling with disdain. He cleared his throat, lifted his glass in a gesture of dismissal, and pointed toward the stairs. His expression was unyielding, leaving no room for argument.

"Aurelia… Septima… go make yourselves presentable and come introduce yourselves to the men you will marry."

Aurelia's lungs lost their ability to expand, and she saw the same expression of dread twist her sister's face. Their eyes locking for only a moment, Septima wrapped her arms around her chest, and the sisters forced their feet upon the steps. They climbed the steps as though ascending a scaffold, each creak beneath their feet tightening the noose around their throats. Instead of heading to her own chambers, Septima followed Aurelia.

"I can't do this, Lia," Septima said as she pulled her filthy clothes over her head. Not waiting for a response, she scurried through the bathing room that separated their chambers to grab a suitable dress. "I will not marry that man."

Heart hammering against her ribcage, Aurelia stepped out of her trousers, tripping over the fabric as her chaotic thoughts whirled. "I know. We'll figure this out. I promise. But we have to go back downstairs. We can't just disobey him."

Septima grimaced as she tied her dress into place, ignoring her disheveled hair, and walked toward the door. With no other choice, Aurelia followed.

Stumbling down the stairs to the strangers whom her father had promised them to, Aurelia held her sister's hand, silently begging for a way out, but Aurelia knew prayers to the gods could not help her. If their father wanted them married, then there was no way for them to get out of that arrangement.

Already at the dining room table, Proteus and the two men chatted amongst themselves, glasses of brown liquor reflecting the firelight in their hands. Both men looked to be in their late twenties, nearly a decade older than their potential brides, but that wasn't uncommon in Vaekros. The sisters took seats opposite their suitors, with Proteus at the head of the table—a king in his castle. His face was carved from stone, void of humor or patience. The warning in his eyes told them clearly: objections would not be tolerated.

Aurelia glanced at the vacant chair opposite their father—her mother's chair. Fifteen years had passed, yet the emptiness at that place still hollowed her chest. She had dreamed of her mother at her wedding, of learning from her how to cradle children and keep a family whole. Instead, servants had raised her, and cold marble halls had become her cradle.

Their mother, Messalina, had succumbed to the plague. Their father, having been away on campaign in a foreign land, was not infected. Aurelia and Septima, only children then, were also spared, kept away at the first sign of illness. Aurelia wasn't allowed to watch her mother waste away, a fact that comforted her. She'd loved her mother dearly and was glad to keep the memories of her mother's beautiful face in her mind, not her deathly visage. Still, it left Aurelia without closure. She'd never been given the chance to say goodbye.

"Aurelia," Proteus said, interrupting her thoughts. "I'd like you to meet Philo."

The man directly across from her dipped his head in acknowledgement as a half-smile spread across his face. "Nice to meet you," he said.

"And you," she responded, forcing a smile of her own, although she knew it did not reach her eyes.

Philo was handsome, but he was at least five years her senior. Sandy blond hair swept across his forehead but was pulled back into a tie at his nape. His eyes, the color of summer grass, eased her nerves ever so slightly. She didn't want to marry him. She didn't even know him, but she was relieved that he at least appeared to be kind.

"Septima," her father said, motioning to the other man. "I'd like you to meet Caius."

Septima's face drained of color, her lips pressing into a thin line as her eyes flicked toward Caius. It wasn't rudeness, Aurelia knew it was revulsion she could not hide. He greeted her kindly, but Septima wore her rejection on her face. It was something their father would not miss. After breathing what appeared to be a hello, Septima reached for Aurelia's hand below the table. Lacing their fingers together, Aurelia ran her thumb over Septima's trembling hand, hoping to soothe her nerves. The air in the room was suddenly too thin as she struggled to inhale.

Dinner was brought out as Aurelia and Septima sat in silence, the meal seeming to go on without them. Roasted duck and vegetables were placed in front of them, as well as a tomato and cream bisque. The soup was Septima's favorite, but she didn't accept the bowl when Aurelia pushed it toward her. Aurelia ate a small amount of each dish. Still, she had lost her appetite after being accosted at the door by their father with unwanted engagements.

Not taking a moment to acknowledge his daughters, or even ask about their day, Proteus rambled on with the men, discussing business and political matters. Aurelia sat quietly, more out of place in her own home than she'd ever been, jaw tense as she waited for her father to dismiss them from the table. It wasn't as though they were needed in the conversation anyway, not even when it involved their own lives.

Septima's hand continued to grip Aurelia's, although the tremble had subsided. Aurelia couldn't help but dwell on what her sister was going through at that moment. What would she do if forced to marry a man? Aurelia didn't want to marry a stranger either, but marrying for love in Vaekros was unheard of. Still, it was a dream she had always held in her heart, a hope for their society to change.

Most marriages in their world were arranged for purely political reasons. The potential to gain power and connections was the only thing that mattered. Fathers arranged their daughters' unions, usually as soon as they reached eighteen years of age, to someone who could advance the families' political futures. If the bride's family was of a lower class than the groom's, a dowry would be paid to entice the prospective suitor.

Aurelia didn't know what arrangement Proteus had made with the two men, but she knew he did not need money or political power. She assumed the arrangement was, at the very least, mutually beneficial to the two families. Although she couldn't imagine it would be beneficial to her or her sister. Philo caught her eye several times, smiling kindly at her. Maybe she could grow to love him, but her sister could not do the same with her own betrothed. Even if she could come to care for him as a person, she would never be able to love him as a wife should.

Their father cleared his throat loudly as they finished dinner. Aurelia frowned. Septima's dish remained untouched. Proteus noticed the full plate but allowed the servant to take it away. The scraps would undoubtedly go to Kano, who was sleeping in the bedroom upstairs.

Rising from the table, her father lowered his eyebrows and leveled them with a stern look that left no room for argument.

"Well." He reached over to shake the suitors' hands. "I have some work to do in my study. Lydia will bring out dessert. Girls," he said, looking at his daughters. Aurelia's stomach tied in a knot as she hung on to Proteus's following words. She didn't want to entertain the men, although it didn't appear she had a choice. She held Proteus' gaze as Septima dropped her head and rubbed her eyes. "Get to know these fine young men. I'll be in my study if anyone needs me."

Dipping his chin to the men he'd selected for his daughters, their father strolled out of the dining room, heading toward the stairs.

Once he was gone, and although it would infuriate him, Septima rose from the table without warning and dashed out of the room, leaving her betrothed at the table, his mouth falling open as he watched the empty doorway. Having already ascended the stairs, Aurelia knew there was no way he wouldn't see Septima with his study being so near their chambers, and she knew he wouldn't be so forgiving.

Murmuring an apology to the men, Aurelia left them in the dining room alone, leaving the room to look for her sister.

A loud clap echoed around her as she took the stairs two at a time. The slam of Proteus' study door echoed behind her like the crack of a whip. Aurelia's pulse still thudded with the fear that he had seen Septima flee, and that punishment would come swiftly.

When she opened the door to her bedchamber, she found Septima curled up on her bed, sobbing into Kano's fur. The massive feline looked up as Aurelia entered the room, but Septima's eyes never lifted as sobs wracked her frame, her fingers curling into his striped fur.

Crawling onto the bed, Aurelia folded her body around her sister's, wrapping her in an embrace.

"Are you okay?" Although Aurelia knew Septima wasn't okay, she didn't know what else to say. Proteus didn't have to hit her, but he did a lot of things he didn't need to do. Without their mother's light, his heart had grown dark. He'd never remarried, never dated. His wife had been his everything, and without her, he'd become a shadow of who he once was.

"I can't do this, Lia." Septima's voice hitched as she spoke into Kano's fur, her throat bobbing. Unsure of what to say or do to ease her pain, Aurelia squeezed Septima's arm.

"I know, sissy. I just don't know how to fix it."

Rolling onto her back, Septima stared at nothing, tears trailing down her beautiful face as the mark from Proteus' hand began to turn purple on her cheek. She continued to pet Kano, the motion seeming to be more to soothe herself than him.

"I can't stay here. I can't let him do this to me. I don't know where I'll go, but it won't be here."

Aurelia swallowed around the lump of emotion in her throat. "What do you mean? You can't... but..." Although her mouth continued to move, Aurelia fell silent. Septima turned to face her with unspeakable sadness reflected in her eyes.

"I can't stay here. I won't. I'll run to the forest, a town beyond, I don't care where. Anywhere but here. Anywhere but at his mercy."

Aurelia stewed on her sister's words, trying to make sense of the situation. She couldn't lose her. It wasn't an option. They remained in silence as the sun fell behind the mountains, throwing the room into darkness. When Aurelia finally rose from the bed to light a candle, dangerous thoughts flooded her mind—thoughts she was willing to entertain for Septima.

"I'm coming with you."

Lifting herself onto her elbow, Septima's eyebrows rose. "You don't have to sacrifice your own marriage for me."

Aurelia snorted, returning to bed. "I have always wanted to marry for love, and he's just a stranger. I want to make my own way. I can't do that under Father's thumb."

A mischievous smile crawled across her sister's face. "I said I wanted adventure, but this may be more than we bargained for. Where will we stay? There are creatures in those woods. How will we protect ourselves?"

Aurelia glanced sidelong at Septima before reaching out to scratch Kano under the chin. "As long as we have this big boy, we'll be safe. As far as food, we can pack our satchels with as much as we can carry." Pulling two leather bags out of her armoire, she tossed one to her sister. "We can figure the rest out as we go."

Septima sat up, grabbing the bag and pulling it against her body. "When do we leave?"

Looking at the clear night outside the window, Aurelia turned to face her sister. "Tonight."

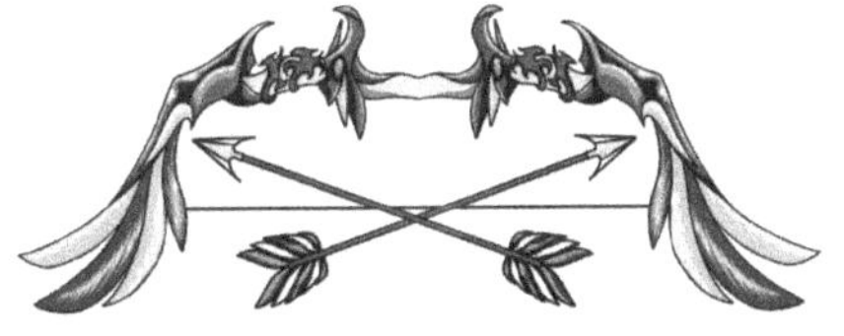

Neither sister had ever stepped beyond their father's shadow, let alone into a world that could devour them whole. But that no longer mattered. It was better to face the unknown than to remain shackled in Vaekros. They would escape—into the forest, into

danger, into freedom. If only they could avoid being caught.

CHAPTER 4

VAEKROS

Sneaking into the kitchens once the servants had turned in for the night, the sisters stuffed their bags with fruits, vegetables, dried meats, and breads. There were wild berries in the forest, and they could learn to hunt if they needed to, but they grabbed what they could to get themselves started. Both strapped their swords to their backs and a dagger around their thighs. They dressed warmly, choosing tunics and trousers and wrapped hooded cloaks over their shoulders.

After returning to take a final look at the bedroom they adored, Aurelia and Septima left the house unnoticed and entered the night air of the back gardens. Both took a fortifying breath and braced for what the forest, and the future, had in store for them. Giving each other a silent nod, they pulled their hoods before they headed for the forest, Kano following stealthily behind. The sisters crept to the tree line in silence, not wanting to chance waking their brother, who lived in the cottage at the edge of the property.

They didn't have a plan other than traveling west through the forest. They knew there were small towns that bordered the forest, as well as larger cities, including El-Wahba, which was where Septima was born. All they knew existed beyond the forest was war-torn cities, none of which sounded like a place they wanted to live. So, they intended, at least at first, to settle in one of the smaller towns, and learn what they could about what else was out there. Both women had gold and silver coins in their bags, money they had saved over the years, and money Proteus would not miss. They hoped they could support themselves, for a time, with what they had.

The dense brush of the Howling Forest took on a more ominous appearance at night. It had been named the Howling Forest for a reason. A menacing howl sounded in the distance as an owl hooted from above. Aurelia gripped Kano's leash so tightly her hand ached as she flinched at every sound. Septima's held a torch that illuminated their way as they traversed the dense branches and vines until it finally opened up to an easier path after several miles.

Knowing they couldn't stop for long, but too exhausted to go any further, they stopped in a thicket to rest. Their father would undoubtedly begin a search to look for them after he had servants scour the extensive property. They had little time to rest, but they could afford to sleep until at least first light. They built a small fire and backed themselves against the trunk of a hollowed-out tree. Septima took the first watch while Aurelia attempted to sleep. Kano remained on high alert while they sat in the darkened forest. Aurelia leaned back against the great cat, closing her eyes and waiting for unconsciousness to consume her.

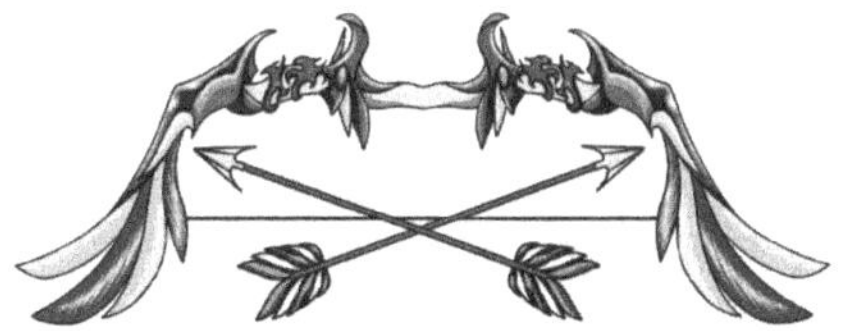

Tendrils of mist recoiled in front of her, beckoning her forward like the inward curl of a finger. Its invitation was seductive, alluring, but the path was dark. Where was it leading her? She did not know.

"What are you doing here?" The woman demanded as she sat upright in the corner. Her trembling hands straightened the hem of her filthy, tattered dress. Dirt was caked under her nails as though she had tried to claw her way to freedom. "I cannot give you what you want! You're wasting your time."

The man, face hidden in shadows, huffed angrily as he stomped away. "Maybe some more time in the cell will change your mind."

The sparkle of a glittering crown faded into the darkness as the iron door slammed shut. It no longer sat atop the head of the crimson-haired woman, imprisoned in filth. Instead, it floated away in the calloused hand of the stocky man who had stolen her freedom.

Aurelia woke to hands roughly shaking her shoulders, along with the low growling of Kano at her side.

"Lia, someone's coming. Wake up." Septima crouched beside her, whispering in her ear. Rubbing her eyes and shaking off the strange dream, she sat upright and peered into the distance.

"What's going on?"

"The branches cracked, and I heard voices. I put the fire out, but I think it's too late. They'll see the smoke."

Aurelia nodded as she pulled her legs closer to her body, trying to make herself as small as she could. The faint rustling of trees could be heard in the distance and could almost be mistaken for an animal. But the voices... the muffled voices made it clear people were nearby.

The forest was still black. There was no way to know the time, only that it was somewhere past midnight and before sunrise. It was too late to run. Their footfalls and their inevitable stumbling upon the forest floor would make too much noise for them to escape unnoticed. Their only option was to sit quietly and hope the others would pass them. Aurelia's hands were slick with nervous sweat as her heartbeat thundered in her ears, but they sat still, afraid to breathe as they hoped to remain invisible.

The voices grew closer as the sisters huddled together. Aurelia cringed, clutching at her throat as she realized the people would walk right by their hiding place, and there was nothing they could do about it. Kano's own snarling lowered in volume as if he realized they were supposed to be hiding, and not drawing attention to themselves.

"Do you smell that?" A woman whispered. "Hang on, someone is out here."

The sound of dragging metal slithered through the air, setting Aurelia's teeth on edge. Someone had drawn a weapon.

"Who would be out here?" Another female voice asked. The voice spoke louder, more demanding. "We know someone is out here... no sudden movements... just come out nice and slow."

Eyes wide and with no other solution, the sisters looked at each other. Aurelia grabbed Kano by his leash, and they slowly stood from their place behind the trees.

Two women stood on the trail, only feet from them. They were tall and, although the darkness hid most of their features, the glint of moonlight showed the sword in the hands of the blond woman. Aurelia's stomach did a nervous flip, causing the meager food she consumed to rise in her throat.

"We don't mean any harm," Aurelia said, taking the slightest step back as she reached out and took Septima's hand. "We are just hiding from our father. By the morning, we will be on our way."

The woman who was not holding a weapon, tall with long black hair that draped over her shoulders, tilted her head, eyeing the large tiger at Aurelia's side. "And the beast?" she asked, as she reached toward the handle of a dagger gleaming at her side.

Aurelia gulped, glancing down at Kano before returning her eyes to the women standing before them. "He's not a beast. He's my friend... my pet. His name is Kano. I've raised him since he was a cub. He protects me."

The women looked at each other and lingered for a few agonizing moments, as though they were communicating silently. The same woman spoke. "And when we walk away, you will sic him on us? Have him tear us to shreds?"

Pursing her lips, Aurelia shook her head vehemently. "No, of course not. He's only here to protect me. He will not harm you if you do not harm us."

The other woman, the one with sword in hand, and hair that appeared white in the moonlight, spoke next. "You said you were hiding from your father. Why?"

Septima squeezed Aurelia's hand gently before responding. "Our father intends to marry us off to strange men. We refuse. We are trying to find somewhere else to create a home, to find a place where we can decide our own futures."

The woman snickered. "It's a foolish endeavor. In a world like this, in Vaekros, there is no escaping such a plan. Your father will find you. Women do not have the kind of rights you seek. Not here."

The black-haired woman shot a warning look at her companion. The woman with the sword looked at the ground in a submissive response. There was somewhere else. Aurelia felt it in her bones. She said not here as though there was another place, a place where women had more rights. She chanced to ask.

"My name is Aurelia. This is my sister, Septima." Aurelia lifted her and Septima's intertwined hands. "If you know of a place where we could be free, please tell us." She thought about explaining why Septima could not—would not marry a man—but she did not know of their prejudices, so she didn't.

The woman who held no weapon, clearly of a higher rank, responded first. "My name is Taryn. This is Exie." The woman with the sword nodded. "We knew of a place like that, a place where women had more rights, but it's no longer safe, so it doesn't warrant discussing."

Aurelia frowned. "Where are you from? Are you from Vaekros?" Although it was apparent that the women were not from Vaekros, she still felt it polite to ask instead of assuming.

"We are from a long way away," Exie responded, with no intention of explaining further.

"But you're in Vaekros," Aurelia pressed. "I don't mean to pry. Do you at least know of somewhere safe my sister and I can go? Somewhere we could survive away from our father?"

Taryn arched an eyebrow, looking them both over. "Can you fight?"

Aurelia started, eyes widening as she glanced at her sister. "Fight?"

"Yes. Can you fight? With a weapon? If you can, then I can use you. Maybe." Taryn waited for the sisters' response, shifting her weight and taking a sip of water from her canteen.

Meeting her eyes, Aurelia nodded, as did Septima, but Septima responded. "We train with our older brother. Aurelia trains more, but we both know the basics. We can learn. We will earn our keep. We don't want charity—just a chance to live free."

"There are towns through this forest, but I doubt you would ever make it, even with a tiger. If your father didn't find you first, there are enough beasts in these trees who are the things of nightmares. I do not want your deaths on my conscience. We will take you to our camp, but I'm telling you this once..." Taryn paused, scanning both sisters. "The moment you enter our camp, you cannot return to your old lives. I need to make sure that is something you can handle."

Catching her sister's gaze, Aurelia bit her lip as she weighed their options. She attempted to steady her voice, to fill it with resolve, as she responded. "We will not miss our lives in Vaekros. A part of us will surely miss our brother, but staying here isn't worth losing control of our futures."

Nodding, Taryn held out her hand to Aurelia, and they shook to seal the promise. "Very well. Gather your things. Our patrol is ending, and we must return to camp before first light. We need to move before your father's search parties scour this forest looking for you."

There was not much for the sisters to gather. They had brought barely more than the clothes on their backs and the food they'd stuffed in their satchels, but they collected it. Aurelia wrapped Kano's leash around her hand, petting him gently in assurance, before stepping onto the path to follow the two mysterious women deeper into Howling Forest.

They walked for what felt like hours. Aurelia's legs were weak, threatening to fracture beneath her. The brisk chill of the air wasn't enough to stop the sweat that coated her skin from forming. They walked until night began to fade into day. The light of the sun peeked through the openings in the tree cover, but Exie still held her sword at the ready. Braced for what attack—Aurelia did not know.

As they came upon a clearing, the previously buzzing forest fell silent. Eerie. Finally, sheathing her sword, Exie reached for Septima's hand. Septima stared as if it would bite her. She took a hesitant step back.

Before Aurelia could ask what was happening, Taryn reached for her hand as well.

"If you want to follow us," Taryn said impatiently, "then you'll have to take my hand and trust me. You can't cross the barrier on your own."

"Barrier?" Aurelia asked, confusion clear in her tone. Fear of the unknown weighed on her, making her exhausted limbs heavier.

Exie smirked, waiting for Taryn to explain.

"There's more to this world than what you can see around you, Aurelia. If you want to see our world, you'll have to take my hand."

In an unspoken agreement, the sisters dropped their interlaced fingers and grabbed the hands of the mysterious women before being led through an invisible barrier into a place unknown.

ENJOYING CROWN OF THE PHOENIX?

The Crown of the Phoenix contains multiple books!
Find the Crown of the Phoenix book series here!

https://www.amazon.com/dp/B09RWCCV3Y

If you enjoyed this book, please leave a review!
Reviews are vital to authors! They help books reach
new readers. I really appreciate it!

Leave a review here: https://www.amazon.com/Cro
wn-Phoenix-C-Varian-ebook/dp/B09RWCCV3Y

Sign up for C. A. Varian's newsletter to receive current updates on her new and upcoming releases,
sales, and giveaways:
https://sendfox.com/cavaria

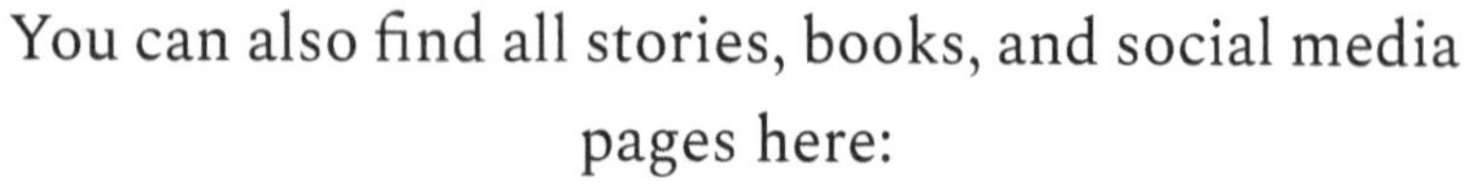

You can also find all stories, books, and social media
pages here:
https://cavarian.com/

ALSO BY C. A. VARIAN

Crown of the Phoenix Series
Crown of the Phoenix
Crown of the Exiled
Crown of the Prophecy
Mate of the Phoenix
Shadowed by Prophecy
Shadowed by the Veil (Coming Soon)

My Alien Mate Series
My Alien Protector
My Alien Rescuer (coming soon!)

Other World Series
The Other World
The Other Key
The Other Fate

Hazel Watson Mystery Series
Kindred Spirits: Prequel

The Sapphire Necklace
Justice for the Slain
Whispers from the Swamp
Crossroads of Darkness
The Spirit Collector
The Darkness that Follows (Coming Soon)

The Cursed Waters Duet
Song of Death
Goddess of Death

Survivor & Savior Duet
Saving Scarlett
Keeping Caroline

Standalones
Second Chance with Santa
When Everly Saved Emerald Hollow (Coming Soon
with A.A. Weaver)
Spirit of the Dying Flower
The Gladiatrix & the Fallen Son (Coming Soon)
Wings of the Forgotten (Coming Soon with J. Paige)

This book would not exist without the people who carried me when I couldn't carry it alone.

To my amazing Executive Assistant, Jessica, thank you for helping me keep my head on straight. You make it possible for me to keep this thing going.

To my incredible PA, Aly Dust, thank you for being a creative force and a constant source of support.

To my awesome editor, Willow Oak Author Services, thank you for keeping up with my crazy schedule.

To my super supportive Street Team, your enthusiasm, love, and loyalty made all the difference. You were the wind at my back through every draft.

To my husband, children, and family, thank you for your patience, love, and for understanding that writing a book means sometimes living in another world.

To my readers, thank you for returning to the page, for believing in haunted girls and broken curses, and for holding space in your hearts for stories like this.

Thank you to my cover designers, Fay Lane and D'Arte Oriel, as well as Leigh Cover Designs for the awesome chapter header design.

From the bottom of my heart, thank you.

XOXO, Cherie

ABOUT THE AUTHOR

Born and raised in the heart of Louisiana's Cajun Country, I'm a passionate writer of dark, fantasy, paranormal, and even alien romances—if there's a romance involved, chances are I've written it. My stories are filled with mystery, magic, and intense emotional connections that keep readers on the edge of their seats.

When I'm not writing, you'll find me creating special editions of my books packed with all the bells and whistles—character art, exclusive swag, and more for my readers to treasure. I love connecting with fans, whether it's through my TikTok shop, my website, or in person at events where I can share the stories I pour my heart into.

proud mother and new grandmother, I've faced many challenges in life, including a battle with chronic Lyme disease, but I've never let it define me. Writing is my escape and my passion, and with the support of my amazing assistant Jessica, my husband Trevor, and my daughters, Arianna and Brianna, I'm living my dream of writing full-time. Even my two youngest sisters pitch in, helping me with various tasks for the business—it's truly a family affair!

At home in the coastal region of Mississippi, surrounded by love, laughter, and inspiration, I'm never without my two Shih Tzus, Charlie and Luna, along with my three mischievous cats—Ramses, Simba, and Cookie. Whether I'm doting on my furry companions, reading, or soaking up family time, every moment is a precious one.

Join me as I continue to create worlds full of romance, adventure, and unforgettable characters that you won't want to put down!